1962

It always rains in Rome

John F. Leeming

It always rains in Rome

Farrar, Straus and Cudahy
New York

Contents

Contents

I

The Mayor

T HEN," SAID ROBERTO SADLY, "I THINK YOU ARE
most unkind. You are married to my dear sister,
Lisetta, and it is from you that I should receive
consolation and sympathy."

"I am not unkind," replied Arnaldo. "It is not my
nature to be without sympathy—I am always consoling
others. That is well known by every one."

"I asked you what you thought might happen to me
when the Tedesci left, and you said——"

"I said, the beastly British would undoubtedly put you
against the wall in the square, the long wall with the so
beautiful cornice on the top, and would shoot you. It is
not unkind to say that, it is the truth. You ask me and I
say, without doubt, they will shoot you."

Roberto flung up his hands.

"I do not believe you. I shall explain to the beastly
British, I shall tell them I have always been on their side.
I shall say that as the Mayor of Fontana d'Amore I have
behaved most correctly. I shall say——"

"And what do you think Tommaso Ucelli will say?"

"Ucelli! That avowed Communist! A man who is now
hiding in the hills, afraid to show his face. A man who
dare not come into his own town in case the Tedesci
recognize him. A detestable coward skulking . . ."
Roberto paused, then added thoughtfully, "Perhaps, when
the Tedesci leave, it might be wise for me to take to the
hills for a time. Yes, I could always do that."

"It might be wise," Arnaldo agreed. "For undoubtedly Tommaso will proclaim that you have been a Fascist, a leading Fascist, for more than fourteen years; that you went to Rome and received a decoration from the Duce; that when war was declared the Party made you mayor because of your unshakeable loyalty."

Roberto took a long drink from the flask of wine.

"It may be the Americans that will come," he said thoughtfully. "If so, everything would be easy, I should tell them of my many friends and relations in America. They would regard me as an American citizen. The Americans are simple men. They are as schoolboys."

Arnaldo shook his head.

"It will not be the Americans who come—do not deceive yourself. It is the beastly British who will be in this part of the country."

"You are depressing me unnecessarily. It is as I said, you are the most unkind. It may be months before the Tedesci leave. The fighting is still miles away. Anything may happen. The beastly British may never come here."

"I am not unkind," said Arnaldo solemnly. "They will come one day, and they will put you against the wall with the so beautiful cornice. You will see I speak the truth. You may hide in the hills for a time, but remember Tommaso Ucelli knows the paths, knows every rock and bush, he has been hiding in those hills ever since Russia attacked Germany. One night he and his gang will catch you. You will find yourself surrounded, you will see them closing in on you. Then it will be the wall with the so beautiful cornice, and—*crack, crack*—it will be all over."

Roberto stood up.

"Then," he said, with impressive dignity, "then I

shall have died for my country. One day there will be a great plaque in the square, perhaps even a statue in bronze, with the imperishable words upon it: Roberto Conti, who gave his life for his country——"

"I do not think so," Arnaldo interrupted, "for you will not have died for your country. The reason why they will shoot you is that you are a Fascist and have been one so long. That is not dying for your country, it is simply that you are on the wrong side. I have always said it would come, every time I saw you swaggering along in that great black shirt, every time I heard you making those speeches at the meetings and at Dopolavoro I said to myself, I said, 'Roberto Conti, like the egg on the wall, will one day find himself in pieces.'"

"I do not wish to listen to you," replied Roberto, "I will go. I came to discuss my problems, but it is as I say —you have not been helpful. You have depressed me. Yes, I am more depressed than when I arrived. I will now leave you, Arnaldo."

"Buona sera," said Arnaldo pleasantly.

Roberto walked out across the farmyard and, skirting the haystack, turned off into the narrow lane. He walked slowly, for although it was nearly evening, the air was still hot, and—a stout man—he had long ago learnt the discomfort that hurrying brings. Down the steep slope of the lane he strolled towards the small town—really, Fontana d'Amore was more a village than a town.

In spite of his unsatisfactory conversation with Arnaldo, Roberto was not feeling unduly worried. Arnaldo had one of those logical minds. He put two and two together and made it four. He was not kind. Arnaldo did not foresee the ingenious explanation Roberto could make to the British, if they ever came. There were so many things to be said. That he had been a Fascist could not be denied, but in his heart he had always hated Fascism. He had accepted the nomination as mayor because he was an honest man and felt that as Mayor of Fontana d'Amore he could minimize the evils of the regime. If there were people who said that since the Tedesci had come he had worked for them, that was untrue. He had had no option. It was well known what the Nazis did to mayors who refused to assist them. No one disliked Germans as much as he did. Think of the insulting things Von Goslar had said to him. And that sergeant, Sergeant Speidel—could anyone have been more discourteous?

Besides, the beastly British might never come. The Nazis seemed to have large forces and much of everything they required. Possibly the war would come to a standstill; then one day they would have to make peace, and all these barbarian armies would go home.

As he strolled slowly onward Roberto began to look happily at the valley below; its beauty soothed him. Although he knew it all so intimately, he was always conscious of the beauty of Fontana d'Amore. The pale grey mountain-peaks against the clear blue of the cloudless sky; the soft grey of the olive-trees on the lower slopes; the low stone walls forming terraces, terraces that rose like shallow steps up the hillsides, so that every inch of soil could be cultivated; the precious earth that had been gathered basket by basket and carried up the hillside bit by bit, the toil of countless generations of peasants; the vines on their frames, like pergolas, protecting the small plants beneath.

Roberto looked dreamily at the pink-washed houses; at the swinging bell in the campanile, the bell that centuries ago had been shining brass, now weathered by sunlight

and rain to a sombre grey. He looked at the foaming
torrent of the river that flowed through the valley. And
finally he looked down at the bridge, with its ancient
stone arches, that joined the two cliffs at the end of the
village.

The beauty of this place he loved soothed Roberto
like a caressing hand.

"*You have been where?*"

Roberto leapt as if he had been touched with a hot
iron. Occupied with his thoughts, he had not seen the
Nazi sergeant approach. The menacing creature was within a yard of him.

"I have been searching for you," snapped Sergeant
Speidel. "You have been where?"

Roberto had loathed Sergeant Speidel when he had
first met him, and time and better acquaintance had done
nothing to change Roberto's feelings. The sergeant was
so massive, so muscular, so aggressive. Roberto disliked
his harsh voice, the way he shouted, and his domineering
manner. An unpleasant bully.

"Ah, buon giorno, my sergeant, it is with much
pleasure that I meet you. You have been walking, you
look hot; perhaps a glass of wine with me——"

"I have looked everywhere for you," said the sergeant,
totally ignoring the offer of wine. "You will come."
Then he added slowly and impressively, "The commandant will see you."

There was a finality in his tone as he made this statement. It was as if, thought Roberto, the sergeant were
Saint Peter in a rather bad temper, opening the gate of
heaven to some person with an unsatisfactory record, and
announcing ominously, "God will see you now."

"It will be a pleasure for me to see the commandant;

for Colonel von Goslar I have much affection. Yes, certainly I will come; I will make it convenient to visit him to-morrow."

"You will come now," said the sergeant grimly. "My orders are to bring you to him. You have already wasted much time. Come! March!"

He did not grip Roberto's arm, but as the two men stepped forward it seemed to Roberto that if he were not actually under arrest it amounted to much the same thing. It was clear that if he did not accompany the sergeant willingly he would be taken forcibly.

"I hope," he said nervously, "there is nothing wrong?"

The sergeant strode on unheeding.

"For Colonel von Goslar I have, as I said, much affection, and respect. What does he want to see me about?"

"You will learn."

"But for what reason does he want to talk to me? If we are to discuss——"

"My orders are to bring you to him. It is not for me to tittle-tattle with every roadsweeper—that would not be correct."

For perhaps fifty yards they marched in silence.

It was intolerable, decided Roberto. Here was he, Roberto Conti, Mayor of Fontana d'Amore, he who had been decorated by the Duce, treated by a common sergeant as if—— It was abominable, it was discourteous. He would stand it no longer, he would revolt, he would——

"Not so fast, sergeant," he panted, "it is humid, and I am not accustomed to this pace."

"It would be better for you if you were. The fat on you would be taken off."

Seething with resentment, Roberto trotted on, until

they reached the outskirts of the small town. Then they
turned down a narrow street, little more than an alley,
where the brightly coloured houses, crowding forward
on each side, gave shade from the vivid sunlight at midday. At last, near the bridge, they reached a larger building that had recently been repainted, a building that
somehow seemed different from the others. Its wide stone
steps were spotlessly clean, its window-sills unhampered
with the usual bird-cages and washing hanging out. Over
the big double doors was a large swastika.

Up the steps the sergeant hurried, shepherding the reluctant Roberto before him, and through wide doors into
an entrance hall, in which five or six men in grey uniforms were at tables busy writing. The sergeant strode
briskly across the hall and started to open a door at the
far end.

"In here you will wait——"

He broke off suddenly as Roberto's foot slipped on the
highly polished floor. It was only by a quick grab at the
sergeant's arm that Roberto managed to regain his balance.

"Now, you are up to what?" snapped the sergeant,
shaking himself free.

"It is abominable! These floors are unsafe! You have
made them so, polishing and polishing until they are like
a mirror——"

"It is not the floors that are at fault; it is the bad wine
you have been drinking."

The sudden slip had shaken Roberto. He turned on the
sergeant in a fury. "Do you think an Italian does not
know how these floors of tiles should be treated? You
Germans do nct understand; you polish them foolishly,
until a goat could not walk upon them. You will have

accidents. You will break bones. In Italy we sweep the dust from the tiles. We do not——"

The sergeant cut him short. He was not going to waste his time arguing about the right way to treat floors. "Italians are not hygienic. You are—how do you say it?—*immondo*, unclean. Dirt and untidiness you accept; we do not." Then, opening a door leading into a small room, he continued, "Go in. In there you will wait. I now go to tell the commandant I have caught you. Inside with you!"

Roberto found himself in the small room. The door closed. A key clicked in the lock. He was alone. "I tell you those floors are dangerous," he shouted. "You polish that which was never meant to be polished. You are fools and you do not know it. You will break bones——" A happy smile crept over his face. The pleasant thought had come to him of the sergeant with many, many broken bones.

Roberto looked around the room; it was a bare, empty place, with not even a chair to sit upon. The only decoration was a large picture of the Führer on one wall. Roberto glanced at it with distaste; the fanatical eyes in the picture seemed to stare straight through him, menacing, contemptuous. After a brief scrutiny Roberto looked away. In one corner of the room was a large metal desk and a filing-cabinet. Cautiously listening for approaching footsteps, Roberto tiptoed over to the file and pulled at the drawers. They were all locked. He tried the drawers of the desk, with the same result. It is intolerable, he thought, they lock up everything. We are their Allies and they do not trust us, they behave as if——

The sound of feet in the hall outside sent Roberto quickly back to the other side of the room. There was a rattle as the key turned in the lock and the door opened.

"You will come," the sergeant ordered. "The commandant will see you at once."

"Most certainly. Most certainly. It will be a delight——"

"This way with you," said the sergeant, hustling Roberto across the hall and up a broad marble staircase. Then stopping at a door on the landing, he knocked gently. A voice within called "Enter." A moment later Roberto was facing Colonel von Goslar.

"You may go," said the colonel, nodding to the sergeant, who was standing rigidly to attention. Then, with a wave of his hand towards a chair, he indicated that Roberto might sit down.

For perhaps a minute, which seemed to Roberto an hour, Von Goslar stared across his desk, not speaking.

"My dear colonel, you wished to see me. For what purpose I cannot think. It is my hope there is nothing wrong. If so I will put it right without delay. Ever since that so unfortunate affair of the boy who threw stones at the sentry it has been my constant effort to——"

"I sent for you," said Von Goslar.

"Yes, yes, and it was with so much pleasure that I heard you wished . . ." Roberto became aware of the cold, unwinking eyes of the German, and his voice faded away.

"I sent for you at fourteen hours."

What barbarians these Nazis are, thought Roberto. Fourteen hours, when every sensible man, having finished *colazione*, composed his mind and rested. Barbarians!

"I sent for you. You were not at your office."

Von Goslar might be stating definite facts, but there

was an accusing sound in his voice, a tone that made it clear an explanation was being demanded.

"I did not go to my office this afternoon," admitted Roberto. "In my capacity of mayor it was necessary for me to be elsewhere, making many inquiries. I was busy indeed on matters of public importance."

"I want the truth. Where were you?"

For a moment Roberto hesitated. It was possible that he had been watched and that the German knew perfectly well where he had been. "I was at the house of Arnaldo Vivarelli," he replied, "there was much for me to discuss with him."

The German glanced down at a closely typed sheet that lay on the desk before him, a sheet which Roberto thought he had seen before, and which he had good reason to believe was his own record. After a short pause Von Goslar spoke again.

"Arnaldo Vivarelli is your brother-in-law."

"Yes, yes. He is happily married to my dear sister, Lisetta, they have four children who are a great joy to them, while I, never having married, am alone. To be unmarried and not to know the consolation of a dear wife and loving children is great sadness to a man."

Again the German glanced down at the typed sheet on his desk.

"Still, I see that you——"

"That," interrupted Roberto, "is not the same thing. Not the same thing at all."

How he disliked these Germans, thought Roberto. Prying into a man's private affairs. Mentioning things which concerned no one.

"It would be better," said Von Goslar, loudly, "if you

attended regularly at your office. In future you will do so. You understand?"

For a moment Roberto had an impulse to slap this insolent colonel across the face.

"You understand?"

"Yes," muttered Roberto.

It was intolerable. "You were not at your office." Treating him like a schoolboy who had played truant. Prying into his private life. Ordering him about. It was unbearable. Far better than this that the beastly British came. They would not treat him like a schoolboy. They might shoot him, but then he would die gloriously for his country; better that than such discourtesy and humiliation. And in his heart he knew the British would not shoot him; he might cease to be mayor, and for a time life might be somewhat difficult. But that would pass. The sooner the British came, he decided, the sooner it would all be over and life would become normal again. Yes, he would welcome the British in Fontana d'Amore.

"I sent for you," said Von Goslar, "to give you an order. From to-night at twenty hours none of your people will use the bridge. None of them will go within two hundred metres of the bridge. Is that clear?"

"Yes, but——"

"From twenty hours this evening sentries will be posted around the bridge, and they will have orders to shoot anyone seen within two hundred metres. It should not be expected that they will challenge, they will shoot without warning. You will inform all your people of this order. Here is the order in writing. You will now sign that you have received it." Von Goslar held out a buff form. "Sign here."

With a shaking hand Roberto did as he was told.

"It would be well that you let your people know of this order without delay. It is eighteen forty. You have not much time."

"I have no time at all," protested Roberto. "How can I explain to every one in little more than an hour?"

"That is your affair."

"There is no time. It is unreasonable——"

"I sent for you at fourteen hours. If you had been at your office you would have received the order in plenty of time to warn your people. At fourteen hours you could not be found. If my sentries do have cause to shoot anyone it will be due to your inefficiency."

"But——"

"Silence! If you had been attending to your duties instead of sleeping in the sunshine and filling yourself with inferior wine—you see, I know your habits—there would have been ample time."

"That is not very polite," said Roberto, rising. "I will go now."

"Sit down!" shouted the German. "I have not yet finished."

Roberto sat down abruptly. How he disliked these Tedesci, he thought. Why did they not go back to Germany and let decent people live in peace. He had a wild desire to shout "Get out, you pigs!"

"I have something more to say to you," said Von Goslar. "It is this: in a week, or possibly a little more, we are leaving."

It seemed to Roberto he could not have heard aright.

"Leaving!"

"That is what I said. As you know, we have been preparing a new line farther north, and it is now expedient to occupy this line. So shortly you will have to manage as best you can without our help. I am telling you this because it is already no secret. Both the American and the British Intelligence are aware of the movement."

Roberto knew that the joy he felt was showing on his face. He knew that his eyes were wide open, his cheeks puckered with pleasure. He wanted to laugh aloud. With a great effort he controlled himself, and managed to force his face into what he hoped was a doleful expression. "I am desolate," he stammered. "To lose such friends . . . it is terrible. Leaving—you are really leaving?"

Von Goslar inclined his head. "Yes, we are leaving." Then, after a pause, he added, "But we shall come back."

Roberto leapt from his chair as if it had become red-hot. "No, no!" he cried.

"Certainly we shall come back," Von Goslar continued coldly. "That is sure. It may be a month, it may be in a year, it may be in ten years, but return we shall."

Roberto gazed at him like a rabbit fascinated by a snake. He was speechless. To raise his hopes by saying they were leaving, then to smash his joy to pieces by talking of coming back. Was it never to end? Were these Germans and British going to be popping in and out of Italy for ever?

"We shall return. The Führer has said so."

Somehow Roberto managed to murmur something about good friends being always welcome.

"And now," said the Nazi, "you will go and inform your people of the order I have given. They must understand that anyone found near the bridge after twenty hours will be shot without warning. I do not wish to be harsh, but it is necessary, for to-morrow we start putting in the cables and the explosive charges."

"Explosive charges?"

"Certainly. That is essential, because when we are ready to leave we must blow up the bridge."

There was a pause.

"Blow up the bridge!" cried Roberto. "Blow up——You cannot, you cannot, mean it. You cannot. Even you would not do that."

Then he realized from the Nazi's expression that they could and would commit this crime.

"Listen," he pleaded. "You do not understand. Our bridge—it is a thing of beauty—one of the most beautiful things in Italy. It is old, very old. It was built by Taddeo Gaddi—he who was Giotto's godson, he who built the Ponte Vecchio, at Firenze. It is one of the loveliest things in our country. You cannot do this to us. I implore you to listen to me. If you destroy our bridge you will have taken from the world for ever a thing of superb beauty, something that has made generations happy just to look at it, and nothing anyone can do will bring it back again!"

"I do not require you to tell me what is of artistic value. We are a cultured people and our knowledge of art is of the highest."

"You must listen to me," panted Roberto. "Our bridge is beautiful. It is a work of art that cannot be replaced. The whole world will hate you if you commit this crime."

"That is enough. I have told you, when we leave the bridge will be blown up."

"I implore you to listen to me. I will be polite. I must, I must make you understand. Our bridge is like a great painting, like a picture by Michelangelo. It is beyond price. It is something of unearthly beauty. Its lines, its colours! Go, look at it, and you will realize that such vandalism——"

Von Goslar raised his hand. "I realize your feelings," he interrupted. "What you say has already received consideration, and it is with regret that the decision has been taken. I am a reasonable man and so I will explain why the bridge must be destroyed. This valley is steep, the hills are high on each side. The valley makes a formidable obstacle. Destroy this bridge and there is no other route for more than twenty kilometres on each side. An advancing force could be held up for perhaps a week or more. We have no alternative. When we leave for our new line we blow up the bridge completely."

"You cannot, you shall not——"

"Silence! I have been patient with you. Enough!"

Roberto was shaking with fury. All his fear of Von Goslar had gone. The abrupt orders, the insults, the humiliations he had submitted to without daring to protest. But this attitude to a thing so beautiful dashed away his fears.

"Beast!" shouted Roberto. "You shall not! I tell you, we will not let you."

Von Goslar clutched the sides of his desk.

"If your people try to interfere so much the worse for them. We will turn our machine-guns on them, and welcome the opportunity. Now get out!"

"I will not get out! You can shoot me, but you shall not destroy our bridge! You Nazis and your Führer—what are you? I will tell you! Buckets of excreta!"

Von Goslar leapt to his feet and strode to the door.

"Sergeant Speidel!" he shouted. Then, turning on Roberto, he said, "I will not soil my hands on you. You have insulted the Führer. You shall be taught a terrible lesson. My sergeant shall deal with you."

Sergeant Speidel strode into the room, clicked his heels, saluted.

"Sergeant, throw this fool out! Kick him much, and do not be gentle. He has dared to insult the German people and the Führer. Deal with him as he deserves."

The sergeant stepped forward. He was a big hulking brute, taller and much heavier than Roberto. It was as if a powerful gorilla were loosed upon a plump schoolboy. The smile on his face was that of a man who has been given a job he will really enjoy.

As a great paw shot out to grab him, Roberto skipped sideways. The sergeant sprang after him. Roberto ducked. Then as the sergeant leapt again to the attack, his feet slipped. With a startled *"Gott!"* and a crash that seemed to shake the whole building, he fell full length on the polished floor. As he fell, his arms clutching wildly, one hand gripped Von Goslar's leg. The colonel, taken by surprise, off balance, crashed on top of him.

Roberto skipped nimbly over the heaving mass to the open door. For an instant he paused and looked at the grey writhing arms and legs. They reminded him of a newly caught octopus he had once seen on the quay at Napoli. "Yes, buckets of excreta," he shouted.

Then he ran frantically down the stairs, past the Germans sitting at their desks, who looked up, uncertain for the moment, out of the building.

2

The Priest

ROBERTO CONTI RAN SWIFTLY. HE WAS AN ITALIAN, and therefore a realist, so he wasted no time trying to warn the town that the area around the bridge would soon become highly dangerous territory. Knowing the people of Fontana d'Amore as he did, Roberto felt sure that the glimpse of a German sentry on the bridge would cause them to keep well away, and that if a shot were fired the crack of that shot would be a far better general warning to the townspeople than anything their mayor could organize.

Roberto Conti trotted alertly down the narrow street that led from the German headquarters, listening for sounds of pursuit. Down an alley, with tall buildings pressing close on each side, he ran—an alley that sloped so steeply it seemed difficult to believe that even a mule could keep its feet on the cobbled roadway—under an ancient stone arch crowned by a statue of Our Lady, and out into the square.

There were many people around the square: three stout women dressed in shabby black, gossiping outside the fruit shop; an even stouter woman near the kerb, sitting on a stool beside a huge basket of flowers; four or five boys playing noisily, their game watched by a few more children who stood silent in the different doorways; a tired-looking, ill-fed, scraggy horse, drooping between the shafts of a battered grey cart; and through the open glass doors of a barber's shop some men were being shaved.

Roberto ignored it all. He fled across the square towards the church, with its grey façade carved and decorated. Then, with a guilty look over his shoulder, he swung into the passage beside the church. A moment later he was knocking at the door of the presbytery. He knocked twice more before he heard the stumbling footsteps of the old woman who was housekeeper to Don Leone. Then the door opened, grudgingly, a few inches.

"Let me in, quick," said Roberto.

The old woman saw who the visitor was and immediately started to shut the door.

Roberto pushed his foot between the frame and the door. "I cannot stand here," he protested. "Maria, you must let me in."

"You cannot come in. Never did I know such impudence, after the way you have behaved. After what you have said so often about the church, you dare to come here——"

"You must let me in. I must see Don Leone at once."

"I will not have you upsetting him."

"I have not come to upset him," said Roberto indignantly. "I have come to tell him terrible news."

"Then be off and tell it to some one else. You are not coming in here. I know you, Roberto Conti. I knew your father before you were born. He was just the same—talk, talk, talk—a tongue too long for his body."

"I implore you, let me in," pleaded Roberto. "Can't you realize I come as your good friend? If it were not a matter of supreme importance do you think I would soil my reputation by coming here at all?"

"Be off with you, Roberto Conti, go and strut about in your black shirt, go and——"

Footsteps sounded in the passage.

"Don Leone," called Roberto. "It is I, Roberto Conti. I must see you at once. It is vital, more than important. I *must* see you."

"Let him in, Maria," said the priest. "Let him in."

The door began to open slowly.

"It is unwise," grumbled the old woman. "You are being imposed upon. He is a trouble-maker, I know him. He has probably been drinking too much wine. It is a habit of his that is well known."

Roberto stepped through the door into the narrow hall.

"Come this way," said Don Leone.

"Don't trust him," warned Maria. "He once threw stones at my cat."

Don Leone led the way into his study and shut the door.

"Perhaps you will sit down."

Roberto mopped at the perspiration that trickled down his neck. "I have come to give you fearful news," he began. "I know that in the past we have not always agreed, but the situation in which I am now placed is too serious for politics. Something terrible is about to happen. We have no alternative but to unite."

"Tell me," said Don Leone gently.

And Roberto told him.

The priest listened in silence to the long, excited tirade. Only by a nod of his head or an occasional "Ah" did he show that he was following the eloquent recital.

"You are right," said the priest at last, when the

breathless Roberto came to the end of his story. "It is serious, very serious. I am glad you came to me."

"Do not doubt, Don Leone, that they will do as they say. They are without souls, they have no appreciation of the beauty, the great beauty——"

The priest hushed him with his hand.

"There is another aspect," he said slowly. "Have you realized what would happen if they do blow up our bridge?"

"Assuredly. It would fall in pieces into the river, and——"

"Yes, the stones would fall into the river, and the river is very narrow just there; it runs between those two cliffs. It is a gorge, a bottle-neck. There is much masonry in the bridge, which would make a dam. A lake would form."

Roberto's family had been peasants for generations. Peasants who had harnessed the mountain streams bringing the water to irrigate their lands. In a hundred ingenious ways they had tamed the streams, and had learnt how to bring the precious water where it was needed. Roberto knew a lot about hydraulics.

"It would form a lake. It would raise the level of the river, and then—— Why, it would flood the town!" he exclaimed.

The priest nodded. "Much of the town is no higher than the level of the river," he said, "quite a lot of the houses are even lower."

"It is ruin, I see it all clearly," cried Roberto. "If the bridge falls it will most surely block the river, the water will rise, it will pour over the banks down into the town. It would be the end of our homes."

"It is not so much the flooding of the houses I am

thinking about," said the priest slowly. "That is bad enough, but when the block is removed and the river falls again we can in time repair the damage, we can clear away the mud and rebuild. What we cannot bring back is the soil, the good earth, that will have been washed away."

The full extent of the calamity became clear to Roberto.

Land in Italy is precious. Every foot of earth on which it is possible to grow anything is cherished as something vital, for on the produce of the soil the people are dependent. All over Italy the steep hillsides have been scraped laboriously to make terraces—terraces that rise one above the other like steps, each step providing a few more feet of treasured earth. For hundreds of years generations of peasants have toiled, building the retaining walls that make the terraces, quarrying the stone, hauling it up the steep hillsides into position, carrying countless baskets of soil up, to fill the plateaux; and when, as in many cases, soil was unobtainable, creating it from loads of straw, dung, river-sand, and garbage; gathering, climbing, filling, spreading, raking—then back down the steep hillside for another heavy basket.

Fontana d'Amore was no exception. The soil that meant so much to its people had been made by generations of drudgery. Roberto visualized the countless men and women who had spent their working lives building up the fertile earth. And Roberto knew that if the river rose and poured over its banks the rushing water would sweep away the hard-won soil. Most of the stone walls would go too, but that all the soil would be lost was certain.

"I cannot believe," said the priest, "that the Tedesci

understand what would happen. If they realized the destruction of the bridge would also mean the destruction of everything on which the people depend I cannot believe they would smash our bridge. If it were explained to them———"

"You do not know them as I do," moaned Roberto.

"That is very true. You have perhaps known them too well. But it is my duty to try and prevent this disaster, and it is my duty to make it clear to them what will be the consequences of their act. I must go at once and see the commandant."

"He is a snake. He is vile. I tell you I have reasoned with him and failed."

"But I must try. It is our only hope—a faint hope, perhaps, Roberto, but if they were to understand that hundreds of years of work would be wiped out, that the ground would become a desert, the town deserted, that the misery . . ."

Roberto remembered the last glimpse he had of Von Goslar.

"Don Leone," he said earnestly, "I would advise you not to go near that man to-night. When I left him he was angry, most angry. As I told you, I had to defend myself. I had to strike him many times. He shouted for his soldiers to help him; they rushed in—many of them. Had I not fought like a tiger, they would have overcome even me. Don Leone, I warn you, do not go near the Tedesci to-night."

The priest took his hat from a hook behind the door.

"I must go," he said, "I must see the commandant as soon as possible, before he has made arrangements that will be difficult for him to reverse. You will wait for me here, Roberto?"

"I will wait. I am in great danger, but I do not think they would look for me here. I will wait. It is my duty, and however great the risk to myself——"

The priest walked from the room, closing the door behind him. Roberto heard his steps in the little hall, the click of the front door closing.

Roberto waited. At first he looked round curiously, for although in years past he had often been in the priest's study, Roberto had never been there alone, had never had an opportunity of examining it closely. He looked at the numerous small pictures of saints and suchlike subjects that dotted the cream-washed walls. The pictures did not please him, they were mostly coloured illustrations cut from religious magazines, and they seemed to Roberto to be crude and inartistic. An almost lifesize photograph hanging above the red-brick *stufa*—a photograph of Pope Pius XII—provided only a few moments interest. Although not fond of reading—normally he read little but *Giornale di Italia*—Roberto inspected the priest's books. Here again he found nothing which he considered would occupy his troubled mind: a New Testament, a breviary, various devotional books, and some volumes on theology. Roberto sat down in the battered old armchair with its threadbare red covering that had once been red velvet, and waited.

He thought of the beautiful bridge he had known as long as he could remember anything. He thought of his mother once telling him it was on this bridge, when she was a girl, that his father had first spoken to her of marriage. He remembered how his mother, coming back from the town, would pause for a little while, leaning over the parapet to watch the rushing stream below; and how after his father had died she would not cross by the bridge, but would walk more than a mile farther on, to where it was possible to cross the stream by the stepping-stones.

Then he wished that so many of the springs in the priest's armchair were not broken, and also regretted that there was a castor missing.

Roberto waited. Nearly an hour and a half went by before he heard shuffling steps in the hall and the door of the study opened.

"Roberto Conti," said the old woman, "how long do you intend to stay?"

Roberto waved her aside.

"I am waiting for Don Leone. He asked me to do so. You heard him yourself."

"Never mind what I heard, Roberto Conti, it's time you were off. Never did I know such impudence, coming here, and sitting here like a duke. Be off with you!"

"Don Leone asked me——"

"Don Leone, when he comes back, will be too tired to talk to you. Not that he will get much chance of talking, poor soul. I know you; it is you that will do all the talking. Too often I've heard you shouting and ranting in that black shirt of yours. Be off!"

"Do you think it is any pleasure for me to be here?" demanded Roberto, springing from his chair. "Do you think I want to be in a priest's house? What do you suppose people would say if they knew I was here?"

Maria waved her hands. "And what do you think the Pope would say if he knew you were thrusting yourself on poor Don Leone?" she said.

"That Pope! That Pope indeed! I'd like to see him try to say anything to me. Every one knows the Vatican is full of escaped prisoners, full of beastly British and

Americans. What about that Irishman, that Father O'Flaherty? It is well known that he is always helping and comforting escaped prisoners—an Irishman disgracing his country in that way! And what does that Pope do about it? He does not, as he should do, shoot this Father O'Flaherty. No, he makes him a Monsignore. I read all about it in *Giornale di Fascism*. Moreover, the Vatican is the only place in Italy where you can get white bread. White bread at a time like this! I tell you, that Pope, he should be stopped!''

Before the angry old woman could launch the devastating reply that trembled on her lips there came the sound of the front door opening. Don Leone had come back.

"Well?" cried Roberto.

"It was useless," said the priest. Then, crossing the room, he sank into the chair Roberto had recently vacated. "It was quite useless. I almost think I did more harm than good."

"Was I not right? Did I not warn you that the Tedesci would not listen. I said to myself when I saw you leave so confidently, I said, 'Don Leone is wasting his time.' ''

"Take no notice of him," put in Maria, "he has been drinking too much wine. I can smell his breath."

"At first," said the priest slowly, "they would not let me in. It was only with great difficulty that I persuaded them to hear me at all. When I did reach the commandant he was not courteous. He kept shouting that it was an order, as if he felt that ended the matter. I did my best to make him understand that if he blew up our bridge the town would be flooded and so much of our precious soil, the work of hundreds of years, would be lost. He was not courteous." He paused, then after a moment went on speaking. "Roberto, I have been unfair to you, and misjudged you, and it is my duty to tell you that I am sorry. When you said to me you had fought with the Tedesci I did not believe you. I was wrong and I confess it. You must have fought with great bravery. It was clear there had been a serious struggle. The German sergeant had a long strip of sticking-plaster across his nose, and the commandant's eye was swollen and highly coloured."

"Ah, Don Leone, you do not know me. When I am enraged I become a tiger. I sweep through my enemies, I destroy them without mercy, I am fearless."

"Rubbish!" Maria intervened. "Never did I hear such rubbish!"

"The Tedesci are very angry," the priest went on hurriedly, "very angry. Your name was mentioned, and the commandant said . . . Well, what he said was discourteous. I do not think you should return to your lodgings to-night. It would not be safe for you to do so. If the Tedesci were to find you . . ."

"You think," began Roberto, "you think . . . You don't mean they would—would shoot me?"

"No, no, I feel they would not do that. From what the German sergeant said, I think it probable they would kick you severely; kick you before the townsfolk, backward and forward across the public square."

"That would be good for him," said Maria. "The Tedesci have more sense than I thought."

"Believe me, it would not be wise to return to your lodgings to-night. I think you had better sleep here."

"Mia Madre!" cried the old woman, "Roberto Conti sleep here? What next! You do not know him, Don Leone."

The priest silenced her.

"So sure was I that it would be unwise for you to return to your lodgings to-night that as I passed I called in and told Luigi not to expect you."

"That was unnecessary," Maria snorted. "Luigi is accustomed to Roberto Conti returning home in the early hours of the morning."

"We must find you a bed here," said the priest firmly. "Maria, have we any sheets?"

"Sheets! And he is to have the room the holy bishop slept in, I suppose? Roberto Conti sleeping in the same room as that saintly bishop——"

"There is no other room," said the priest, "I am sorry to cause you trouble, Maria, but will you now go, please, and prepare. I ask you as a favour to me."

The old woman hesitated. "Will any of us be safe in our beds with Roberto Conti in the house?" she asked. Then, as she turned and went through the door, she added, "For me, I shall lock my door." She closed the study door, then opened it again for a moment and added, "I shall also wedge a chair under the handle."

After she had gone the two men sat in silence.

"I am sorry," Don Leone said. "You should try to forgive Maria. She means no harm."

Roberto did not reply. He was thinking of the bridge, the beautiful bridge he had known all his life, the bridge his mother had loved so well. And these vandals, these horrible Tedeschi would blow it into little pieces. He could almost hear the roar of the explosion, almost see the stones flying upward against the sky, then falling, tumbling down into the river—the great splashes as the masonry fell into the water, the sliding, tippling stones; and then the river checked by the fallen rocks, the water beginning to rise, a pool forming, the pool spreading; the first trickle of water over the bank, the trickle growing, faster, faster, then with mighty force sweeping all before it down into the town below.

"They shall not do it!" he cried. "No, no! We will fight them. We will not allow this crime."

"We cannot fight them," said the priest. "They are organized, well armed, and ruthless. If you incite our people to resist they will be mown down. We should not have a chance."

Roberto knew that what the priest said was true. "But there must be something we can do," he urged. "Are we to sit unmoving while they bring ruin on the whole town? You, Don Leone, as a priest, must turn the other cheek, but for me it is intolerable. We should fight."

"It would be useless bloodshed. We have no arms. It is only a few months ago that you, Roberto, on the instructions of the Tedesci, ordered all our people to hand in even their shot-guns. By your orders the people are now disarmed."

"I am not sure if that is so, Don Leone. It is possible that some of them did not obey the order as they should have done. I have reason to think . . . Several times I have intended to inquire more fully, but always something has kept arising to occupy my attention. Since the Tedesci came I have had so many things to attend to. It has been 'See to this,' 'Do that,' 'Why did you not?' . . . Oh, it has been awful."

"Roberto, I will not agree to our people being encouraged to fight the Germans—at least, openly. It would be futile. The Tedesci would burn the town. They would take hostages. They would shoot them."

There was silence for a few moments. Roberto thought of the disaster that was to come upon them—the bridge, the floods, the precious soil swept away; and twice Don

Leone seemed to be about to say something, twice he hesitated.

"Roberto," he said at last, "Roberto, do not misunderstand me. I realize fully—better than you, perhaps—that if the bridge is blown up it will be the end of our homes. If by giving my life I could prevent this I would do so, but it would not be just my life, it would be many others, and we should achieve nothing."

"So we watch them bring ruin——"

"What I am saying is that our people cannot fight the Germans; it would be madness. How many young men are there left in the town now?"

"Half the young men," said Roberto bitterly, "are skulking in the mountains with Tommaso Ucelli."

"That is what I am trying to tell you. We cannot fight because nearly all the fit men are with the partisans. The men who are here are old and untrained. We have no arms. But in the mountains there are young men, men who have had training in the army, men with good rifles. It is they who may save the town. Roberto," the priest ended solemnly, "we must put the case to Tommaso."

Roberto leapt as if he had received an electric shock. "Tommaso Ucelli? that Communist! that creature?" he cried. "I would rather die a thousand times."

"That Tommaso is a Communist is true, but at heart he is not a bad man. He is misguided, he does not at times see things in their true perspective, and being proud, he is unwilling to admit his mistakes. Remember, I have known him all his life; I baptized him; he was at our school here, and I gave him his First Communion. I know Tommaso, and I tell you he loves Fontana d'Amore."

"That I should live to hear a priest of God talk in this way! An avowed Communist!" Then, remembering something the old woman had said earlier in the evening, Roberto added, "And what do you think the Pope would say if he could hear you?"

"I think the Holy Father would say, 'Don Leone, like you I detest Communism, but Tommaso has trained men in the mountains, men with guns and ammunition. It may be that he can help, and as there is no one else to whom you can turn——' "

"And how," interrupted Roberto, "are we to find this wonderful Tommaso? Do you know that the Tedesci gave orders months ago that he was to be arrested? Do you know that I instructed the Carabinieri to find him. Has anyone seen a trace of this creature? No, certainly not! He is hiding in the hills, and not a soul has had a glimpse of him. Even if we wanted to, how are we to get in touch with him? That is what I ask you. Tommaso indeed! Well, I say to you, where is he? Find him, that is all I ask. Find him. Do you think you can find him when the Tedesci and I and the Carabinieri could not do so?"

The priest hushed him with a gesture of his hands. "Gently, gently, Roberto," he answered quietly. "Of course we can find him; in fact, I have already done so."

"By running about the hills shouting 'Tommaso,' I suppose."

"For a man in your position——forgive me, I do not mean to be unkind—you are singularly ill-informed. Don't you know that Tommaso visits the home of Francesca Camerata at least twice a week? They are very much in love, and will be married as soon as this terrible war ends."

Roberto snorted. "Why was I not told of this? If what you say is true the Carabinieri must have known."

The priest shrugged his shoulders. "Perhaps they did

not try very hard," he replied. "Perhaps in these uncertain times they felt it best to wait until to-morrow. However, I called at the Casa Camerata on my way from seeing the German commandant. I spoke with Signora Camerata; they were expecting Tommaso at any minute; I asked them to tell him I needed to speak to him on a matter of the greatest importance."

"And so," said Roberto cuttingly, "I suppose he is coming here. An avowed Communist hobnobbing with a priest of God. Let us get out the wine, let us――"

There was a slight sound in the passage, a sound of footsteps. The door opened. Tommaso Ucelli stepped into the room.

"Ah, Don Leone――" he began, then as he caught sight of the Fascist mayor, he stopped suddenly. His hand went swiftly to his pocket.

3

The Partisan

IS THIS A TRAP?" DEMANDED TOMMASO. HIS HAND came from his pocket holding a small automatic. "If this is a trap——"

"Do not be foolish," said the priest calmly. "You know very well I should not deceive you. Put that pistol back in your pocket."

"Then what is that slob"—Tommaso pointed at Roberto—"doing here?"

"Roberto and I must talk to you. Something disastrous is likely to happen——"

"So I am to be called a slob, am I?" interrupted Roberto. "Let me tell you, Tommaso Ucelli, this day I have fought the Tedesci hand to hand. While you skulk in the hills, I, Roberto, have been fighting desperately with the German commandant and his creatures; many, many of them all trying to kill me, while I raged fearlessly, defying them all!"

Tommaso shook with laughter.

"It is true," said the priest. "I did not believe it myself at first, but to-night I saw the commandant. He did not tell me what had happened, but he was injured and very angry. The German sergeant was even more angry, he had sticking-plaster on his face. Both of them threatened much pain to Roberto when they caught him."

"Yes, I am now a fugitive," sighed Roberto.

Tommaso looked bewildered. He sat down slowly on

the one vacant chair. "I do not understand at all," he said. "You tell me, Roberto . . . No, it is not possible."

"Then I will tell you," said Roberto. "To-day I heard the Tedesci were soon to withdraw to a new line farther north. That did not dismay me, for it is well known how I dislike the Tedesci and how much I would welcome the beas— the British or our American cousins."

"Of all the lies——" began Tommaso.

The priest hushed him with a gesture.

"As I said," continued Roberto, "the news that the Tedesci were leaving was to me welcome, but then I heard other news. It was that when they were ready to leave, when all their forces were across our river, they intended to blow up—to destroy—our so beautiful bridge, to bring ruin on Fontana d'Amore. Without hesitation I hurried to the German commandant, I defied him, I forbade him to be so wanton. He cringed under my wrath, but he refused to obey me. Provoked, I struck him many times. He howled for assistance, his troops rushed in——"

"I do not believe a word of it," Tommaso said. "It is against reason."

"It is true," said the priest, "I have seen the commandant and his sergeant; they were suffering pain and blamed Roberto. Of that I am quite sure."

"But the bridge?"

"That also is true. The commandant made it clear that they intend to wreck our bridge when they move out."

Tommaso's eyes narrowed. He did not need anyone to tell him what would follow the destruction of the bridge. "They are beasts!" he said. "They will destroy the whole countryside, they will bring ruin . . . They are foul, the

whole lot of them! Every German should be extermin-
ated——''

"Not all Germans are bad," intervened the priest soothingly. "Many of them are kindly people, loving music
and children and God. But some of them have become
filled with pride. It is the devil that has got into their
minds, so that they have become boastful and puffed up."

"Like Roberto here. If ever I saw one puffed up with
pride——''

"I sent for you, Tommaso," the priest broke in hurriedly, "because it seemed possible with your aid we
might find a way to avert this disaster. We must think,
we must seek some way to prevent this tragedy."

"What can he do?" demanded Roberto. "An avowed
Communist, who has been skulking in the hills for
months. A creature that hides behind bushes! I suppose
you think he will throw a stone at the Tedesci and they
will run away!"

Tommaso thumped the table with his fists. "Do you
realize that in the hills there are thousands of trained
soldiers, fully armed?" he asked. "Do you know that we
have thousands of escaped British prisoners hiding there;
brave men with the gift of courage? Fearless, clever men,
such as the British Bart. General Sir Neame. Men who are
frightened at nothing."

"If they are so brave and are fully armed," asked
Roberto thoughtfully, "why have they not long ago
come out of hiding and fought the Tedesci?"

"At a signal they will do so. When the proper time
comes I shall give the signal. Then we shall come, not
only to crush the Tedesci, but to avenge ourselves upon
the traitors of Italy. Then we shall settle our scores with
the snakes; the puffed up blackshirts and the priests who

have foisted the opium of religion on the people of Italy."

"Tommaso," said the priest placidly, "you are getting heated."

"Do you realize, Don Leone, that when our day comes we can wipe out the Vatican and the Pope? We can put an end to your whole Church."

Don Leone shook his head. "I am reminded of something Napoleon once said to Cardinal Benuzzi," he replied. "He said, 'I could wipe out the whole Catholic Church. It would cease to exist.' And Cardinal Benuzzi replied, 'If we priests and cardinals have not done that in two thousands years what chance do you think you have?' "

"Religion is the opium——"

"You said that before," the priest interrupted. "You repeat yourself. And you know in your heart you do not mean it. If you were to-night to be hit with a bullet, and knew you were dying, you would send for me. You would ask for Extreme Unction. You would want to make your peace with God."

"Ah, but if I were dying," argued Tommaso, "that would be a very different thing. I could not be expected to risk my soul going to Hell. It would be your duty to come to me."

"I think," put in Roberto, "what he says is reasonable. I myself do not like the Church. Had we won the war, the Duce would undoubtedly have taken over the Vatican. But when a man is near death it is sensible and right that he should take no chances."

"We are getting away from the point," said Don Leone. "What we are now here to find is some way to preserve our bridge, our homes, and our soil."

The Fascist mayor and the Communist partisan were realists. They recognized the priest had stated the real problem. There was silence for a few moments. Don Leone and Roberto looked expectantly at Tommaso.

"Could we . . . No, that is impossible," Tommaso said at last. "The Tedesci are too strong. An open attack is beyond us."

"I could not consent to an attack on the Tedesci," said the priest, "unless, of course, we were sure of success. They would burn the houses, they would massacre our people. It would be ruin for every one here."

Roberto ran his hand across his forehead. "It will be ruin for every one if they blow up our so beautiful bridge," he said.

There was silence for a few moments, then the priest said, "Tommaso, can't you think of anything? If the bridge is blown up there will be floods; the terrace walls will be undermined and will collapse; the soil will be washed away; it will be the end of Fontana d'Amore. I have been wondering if an appeal from the Vatican could help us, but——" He opened his hands in a hopeless gesture.

"I also," said Roberto, "had thought of the Vatican. If I, as the Mayor of Fontana d'Amore, were to stifle my feelings for the good of our people and were to ask that Pope——"

"The Germans would not heed the Vatican in such a matter as this. Gaining time to establish their new line is all that matters to them," Tommaso interrupted. Then suddenly he banged the arm of his chair. "I have it!" he cried. "I see the solution! I have solved it! It is not for us, with a few dozen untrained, half-armed men, to try to stop the Tedesci. It is for the British to do this. It is their responsibility. The Tedesci intend to destroy our bridge—why? Because it is the only sound way across the river for many miles, because they wish to stop the British using this crossing. Then, surely, it is the British who should keep our bridge intact; it is to their interest to do so."

"Or the Americans," suggested Roberto.

"You think the British would send a sufficient force quickly?" asked the priest.

"What I am saying is that it is for the British to save us. If they do not preserve our bridge they will be much delayed, and the Tedesci will withdraw to their new line. This, I tell you, is a problem for the British to solve."

Don Leone nodded agreement. "If they act quickly, yes," he began, "but in the past the British have——"

"They can act quickly when they want. Show a Britisher a good profit and he will not waste time. Once they know the Tedesci mean to destroy the bridge, which is so necessary for crossing the river, the British will be here in no time. It is in their interest to do so."

"It may be worth while," said the priest. "As you say, it is in their interest, and there seems to be no other course."

Tommaso stood up. "I must get a message through at once," he said urgently. "I must return to the hills immediately; I must send a signal——"

"So," interposed Roberto, "it is true you have an illegal radio working in the hills. The commandant was right; he kept saying they had intercepted signals. For more than a week he made my life a misery, demanding that, as Mayor of Fontana d'Amore, I should discover where this radio was placed. I had no rest at all. He wanted me to search every house with Carabinieri. I kept assuring him he was mistaken. He was discourteous."

"We move our radio from place to place. It is never in the same spot for more than a day or so. I must go at once and demand aid from the British. Father Leone, will you go to Francesca and explain I have had to leave on a matter of great importance. She is expecting me to return. If I do not she will take umbrage; she will be moody."

Roberto nodded understandingly. "Lo credo," he murmured. "It is always the same with women. They are not reasonable. They expect too much of a man. I remember a girl——"

"I will go to Francesca Camerata," said the priest. "I will explain as much as is necessary."

Tommaso strode across the room and opened the study door.

"I can save Don Leone a journey," Roberto suggested. "Although as a fugitive I go in danger of my life, I will take your message to Francesca. I will soothe her. Have no worry."

Tommaso paused for a moment. "If I hear you have been near Francesca," he said pleasantly, "I will shoot you in the bowels."

"Buona sera," said the priest.

"Buona sera," replied Tommaso, and, going out into the passage, shut the door.

All the next day Roberto remained hidden in the priest's house. As the day dragged on it seemed to him one of the longest and most unsatisfactory he had ever lived through. It had not started well. He had not slept much during the night, and in the early morning he had been aroused by the sounds of the priest returning from Mass. He had lain in bed pondering about his difficulties until the attractive smell of coffee and the scent of hot rolls had caused him to get up, and, going on to the landing, call down to Maria, telling her to bring up his *prima colazione*. Maria's refusal and the ensuing argument had upset him. All through the day the memory of some of Maria's remarks fretted him. That she should dare to say . . . It was beneath his dignity to accept such abuse from a servant. If he had only thought to reply . . . Yes, that would have wounded her. Why had he not thought of it at the time?

And Don Leone coming out and quelling the dispute, insisting that they both ceased shouting! Even Don Leone's words had added to Roberto's irritation. "Have you no sense?" he had demanded. "Do you want every one to know you are hiding here? Do you want the Germans to know where you are? Do you want them to come here and take you into the *piazza* and kick you hard before every one?"

Later the priest had come and admonished him again. "You must be careful, Roberto. If you are seen or heard the Germans would soon know where you are hiding, and that would be painful for you and bring trouble upon me. Keep away from the window and lower your voice. Always, as a child, you were a shouter."

The long day dragged on. Never a great reader and, in any case, with nothing except a few religious books which were not to his taste, literature did nothing to take his mind off his troubles. There was just nothing for him to do, and while idleness was no hardship to Roberto, at least a bottle of wine and one person to listen to him was essential to his contentment. Regrettably, these were not available.

Several times Roberto could not resist peeping through the window and watching the people moving about in the square. He saw some of them standing in little groups, talking anxiously, and gesticulating. It consoled him to think they might be talking about him, of the gallant fight he had put up against the Tedesci, of his strange disappearance. But there were unpleasant doubts in his mind. He knew the people of Fontana d'Amore and their feelings towards him; if they were gossiping about him it was unlikely they were paying him compliments. It began to annoy him that these people should be out there in the sunshine, talking so freely, while he who was doing so much for the town should be confined alone in the house of a priest.

Maria provided lunch, but set this out on a tray which she left downstairs in the hall, refusing to bring it to him. To add to his annoyance, she came to his room to tell him the tray was below, and by the time the argument between them had finished the *pasta* was cold and the veal chilled and covered with grey grease.

In the afternoon he fell asleep.

Towards seven o'clock Don Leone, who had been out almost the whole day, returned and came up to see Roberto.

"Keep away from that window," he commanded. "If you were to be seen it would be unfortunate for us both, and painful for you. That sergeant—he has been looking everywhere. Twice to-day he has been to your lodgings and—Luigi tells me—searched every room and asked many questions. Yes, you were wise, Roberto, to come here; it is the last place they would expect to find you.

With your record, they would not expect to find you near a church."

"But," replied Roberto, "I have much love for the Church. Why, this evening I even felt a desire to attend Benediction. Then I realized it would not be wise. People would see me there, the Tedeschi might hear of it, and so trouble would fall on you, my loyal protector."

Don Leone smiled. "No, Roberto, it would not be wise for you to be seen at Benediction," he said. Then, after a pause, he added, "But, if you wish, I would gladly hear your confession."

"Confession?" cried Roberto, startled. "There is no need to go to extremes!" Then, realizing this was, perhaps, hardly polite, he added, "Some other time, without doubt—yes, assuredly, some other time."

Don Leone sank wearily into a chair. "I am tired," he admitted. "It has been a trying day."

"And for me, also," complained Roberto. "What with going in danger of my life, and that Maria——"

"I have been seeing as many people as is possible," the priest went on, "soothing and trying to reassure them. It is difficult because I am not sure what is likely to happen and the people are much distressed. Every one in the town and in the country around now knows that the Germans are wiring the bridge—they have been at it all day. It is clear to every one what the Germans mean to do when they leave. I pray the British act quickly."

"And there is no news from Tommaso Ucelli? If you ask me I tell you that man is a windbag. It is my belief he will do nothing. Troppo parlare."

"He has had little time yet. He left us last night about twenty-two hours, then he had to get into the hills to his radio and get a message to the British. Probably they would require a full explanation. It would take some time. No, I do not doubt Tommaso. What I fear is the British wasting time. I know them, they start saying 'I will see what I can do,' which is like us when we say '*domani*,' then nothing happens."

Roberto nodded. "Surely they will lose no time? It is the responsibility of the British to prevent this calamity. As I told Tommaso, it is in their interest to act quickly."

"I suppose we can only wait," murmured the priest, "but this waiting is trying."

There was a pause.

"Don Leone, there is one thing that gives me concern. It is that Maria. Can we trust her? How do we know that she will not gossip—as is her habit. Or how do we know that even now she may be with the German colonel, claiming the reward for discovering me?"

"Maria can be trusted; she will not be indiscreet. She is like the confessional or the tomb. She will say nothing."

"I hope you are right," said Roberto. "But to say nothing would be a change for that one. If you had heard her to-day—the things she said to me. She is without politeness."

"You need not worry. Maria is faithful. No, what harasses me is the fear that the British will be too late. They are our only hope, and the anxiety is wearing me down."

Alone again, Roberto pondered over his problems, Maria—in his heart he knew she could be trusted, but some of the things she had said to him still rankled; he was the Mayor of Fontana d'Amore; and to have a woman, an old, ugly woman like Maria, say such things about him was unseemly. In his life many women had said hard things about him—abuse from feminine lips was no novelty to Roberto—but such upbraiding had come from women who were beautiful—except that old mother of Rosa. One expected a beautiful woman, at some stage, to rave and blame one; it was natural they were disappointed and angry, so they shouted and called one bad names; but for a woman like Maria to do so was insulting.

Roberto sighed. There was his fear about the destruction of the bridge. The bridge was a work of art like a great picture, such as Raphael's *Madonna della Sedia*, and Roberto felt as if he were standing idle while ruffians planned to destroy this thing of beauty. Like a great painting, the bridge was magnificent and unique; there was elegance and grace in its symmetry, the colours in its weathered stones were a joy. Often, when distressed with some annoyance, he had gone to the river bank and sat for an hour or more looking at the beauty of the bridge, then gradually he had become soothed, at peace, happy again. To harm such a lovely thing would be devilish and vile.

However, it could be said his own position had improved. As far as he personally was concerned, his prospects looked brighter than they had done yesterday. Yesterday he had been fearful as to what the beastly British, if they reached Fontaña d'Amore, might do to him. Now a proved enemy of the Tedesci, a man in hiding, sought by the Germans for the blows he had struck, Roberto could not be classed by the beastly British as their enemy. It was reasonable to think they would treat him as an ally. If treated tactfully they might even give him a decoration or an honour of some kind. As far as the British were concerned, he had now no cause to worry—only the worry that they might not come quickly. It was only the Tedesci who were to be feared now, and they were leaving. If he could keep hidden from the Tedesci until they left nothing but good would have come from yesterday's events. And as the priest had said, he was in a safe hiding-place. No one would think to look for a Fascist mayor, an open enemy of the Church, in Don Leone's presbytery. No, he had been wise to come to the presbytery. Trust Roberto to do the prudent thing! He was a man of good sense.

About nine o'clock Don Leone came upstairs again.

"Roberto, you had better come down," he said. "Arnaldo Vivarelli is here."

"Arnaldo! Ah, he will have come to congratulate me on my struggle with the Tedesci. Only yesterday, before I fought with the Tedesci, I went to visit Arnaldo, and he was full of fear for my dangerous position. No doubt he has brought expressions of sympathy from my dear sister."

"You had better come downstairs. But remember to keep your voice low, remain calm."

"Rest assured, Father Leone," said Roberto, with dignity. "I will be cautious. I will do nothing to endanger you who have given me sanctuary."

They went downstairs to the priest's sitting-room, where Arnaldo Vivarelli was waiting.

"Buona sera, Arnaldo, my brother, I knew you would come. . . ." began Roberto.

"I am not your brother," Arnaldo contradicted morosely. "You are my wife's brother. A man cannot help what relations his wife may have."

Roberto ignored the slur. "And my dear sister, Lisetta,

how is she?" he inquired. "She will, I know, be overcome with anxiety on my behalf. Reassure her that I am
so far safe, endeavour to comfort her in her terrible
grief."

"I do not think Lisetta is worrying," remarked
Arnaldo. "What she has kept saying is that you get into
one scrape after another." Then, as if feeling that his last
remark was perhaps not too polite, he added, "But she
did say this time it is not as bad as that scandal about
Rosa. That was a nasty affair. The whole countryside was
talking about it."

Don Leone intervened, "You have come from Tommaso, you have brought news?"

Arnaldo nodded. "Yes, I have news. A British officer
will arrive to-night."

"Only one? No troops or tanks?" asked the priest.

"Only one. Probably he is coming to make plans, to
decide what should be done, then others will follow him.
At least, that is what we hope."

"How will he get here?" Roberto questioned.

"That is no concern of yours. Sufficient that he will
arrive and Tommaso knows where and when to pick him
up."

"Then he is being dropped by parachute?"

Arnaldo ignored the question. He said, "It will be early
morning before he arrives. To-morrow he will no doubt
survey the position."

"I pray he decides quickly," said Don Leone, "and that
the British do not waste time. The moment the Germans
realize the British are behind them, they will blow up the
bridge. It should be a sudden and overwhelming attack
from their rear if the bridge is to be saved."

"Be reassured, father," Roberto said. "The British will

be our saviours. They will drop large forces, irresistible forces, that will crush the Tedesci in one blow. They will save our so beautiful bridge."

"Speriamo."

"I think, Father," said Arnaldo, "you doubt without cause. It is reasonable that they should send only one officer at first; he will decide what is required, and then they will act and we shall be saved. You must admit they have acted promptly once they got Tommaso's message."

"I still say 'speriamo,' " the priest murmured.

"I have no doubts," Roberto intervened. "We are saved, I know it. It is in the interests of the British to stop this dreadful crime. It is to their advantage; you will see they will save our bridge." Then, after a pause, he added thoughtfully, "What I cannot understand is how Arnaldo here comes into the matter. Why has he brought the news? How has he learnt what Tommaso has heard?"

Arnaldo chuckled. "For the Mayor of Fontana d'Amore, for one supposed to be responsible to the Tedesci for security, you are ill-informed. You know nothing," he said.

Don Leone broke in. "I am surprised, Roberto, that you did not know that Arnaldo has been in the Resistance for more than a year. He is second-in-charge under Tommaso. He has done much valuable service."

Roberto sprang to his feet. "Then I have been deceived, grossly deceived, by my own brother——"

"Brother-in-law," intervened Arnaldo.

"——I have been kept in the dark. It is most unfair. It is more—it is discourteous. There was I, harassed by the Tedesci to find these traitors, these so-called partisans, and my own brother could not—well, brother-in-law, then—could not trust me. I tell you I have been treated badly. It is without pardon."

"I thought you must know," said Don Leone. "I thought nearly every one guessed."

Arnaldo laughed. "Why, even the Carabinieri——"

"Then why did they not do their duty?" shouted Roberto. "Can I trust no one? I will not tolerate such behaviour. I will complain. And you, a priest of God, deceiving me in this way! I will complain to that Pope! Has he no sense of right that his priests act in this way? In my whole life I have never known such deception, it is——"

"Lower your voice," ordered Don Leone; "shouting like that, you could be heard in the square. Do you want to bring the Germans here?"

"I will not tolerate . . ."

Arnaldo stood up. "I will go now, Father, it is time I was elsewhere. Then this windbag will go upstairs again and sulk in silence. It will be safer for us if I go now."

The priest nodded.

"Let me tell you, Arnaldo Vivarelli," stormed Roberto, "that you will hear from me again. My own sister deceiving me! I will have respect and trust. As Mayor of Fontana d'Amore I insist upon it. I will . . ."

Arnaldo closed the front door, and Roberto, giving the priest a long, dignified stare, said impressively, "I will leave you to your conscience, Don Leone. For myself, I prefer to be alone upstairs."

4

The Beastly British

IF THE FIRST DAY OF WAITING IN THE PRIEST'S HOUSE
had been trying Roberto found the second one much
worse. Not only did Maria remain surly and con-
tinue to refuse to bring his food upstairs to him, but she
developed a new technique which Roberto found even
more annoying than abuse. When they met she would
say little, but stare at him in a pitying manner.

"They will get you, Roberto Conti," she would say
warningly, "yes, assuredly, they will get you in the end.
I can see it coming. The Tedesci are efficient, they do not
fail to get a man when they want him. Yes, they will
come for you in their own good time."

Such remarks increased Roberto's anxiety.

The long day dragged on, and it was towards evening
when Arnaldo Vivarelli came again to the presbytery.
Don Leone was out, and it was Roberto who took the
message from Arnaldo, Maria standing in the hall, within earshot, and indicating by her manner that she dis-
approved of the whole affair. Arnaldo said little, only
that the friend they were expecting had arrived safely
the previous night, and that Tommaso would be bringing
him to see the priest soon after dark.

"Mia Madre!" Maria exclaimed. "What next! Tommaso, that Communist, coming here again, and the house
already full of lazy Fascists. It is monstrous!"

Arnaldo, although pressed and questioned by Roberto,
would say nothing further.

"I have told you what I know, I have given you the message for Don Leone. That is all that is necessary."

"But," Roberto protested, "there is so much that I need to discuss with you, there are plans to be made, and——"

"No, I must now go home. If I am away long in the evenings Lisetta is inclined to misjudge me unfairly. But then I say to myself, who can blame her for having un-just suspicions, when her own brother has behaved with women——"

"That is what I say," interrupted Maria. "A man who has caused open scandal, not once but many times, thrust-ing himself into the house of a holy priest like Don Leone! I tell you this Roberto here, he lounges about all day long, eating and drinking until one would expect him to burst. He is a nuisance, that's what he is. Why does he not go out and face the Tedesci? That is what I ask. It is what he should do, without doubt. The Tedesci would beat him, and that would be a good thing."

Arnaldo disregarded the heated outburst which Roberto made in reply.

"I will leave you two to dispute in peace," he said. "Arrivederci."

Don Leone returned about an hour later, and Roberto was disappointed at the way in which the priest received the news of Arnaldo's visit.

"But don't you see, Don Leone, we are saved. The so beautiful bridge will not be destroyed by these vandals. It is surely great news. I tell you, now the British are here, all will be well. I myself will soon be free from danger, able to walk out among the people, to receive their congratulations and thanks. Ah, I wonder what that

Maria will feel when she sees me hailed by all? She has again this afternoon been most insulting to me, Don Leone. I do not want to complain, that is not my nature; but that one, she goes beyond bearing, she is——"

"I pray the British have a plan and can act quickly. The Tedesci have to-day finished the wiring and can blow up the bridge whenever they want."

"But, Don Leone, surely you understand that now the British are here they will prevent such sacrilege. It is, as I said, in their interest to do so."

The priest sighed. "We shall have to wait until we hear what the Englishman proposes," he replied. "Time is short. It is being said that the Tedesci are already withdrawing. Certainly more lorries are coming north than are going south."

"Do not distress yourself. Coraggio! I realize that as a priest you must take the gloomy view; that is because you have spent so much time talking about Hell and what will happen to people unless they frustrate their natural inclinations, but I see things more clearly. You may trust me, I am full of hope and courage. Now the British have come, all will be well."

"Speriamo," said the priest.

It was nearly eleven o'clock when, in response to a faint scratching at the window, Roberto gave a startled exclamation, and Don Leone, rising from his chair, switched off the lights, putting the hall in darkness, and opened the street door. Tommaso Ucelli slipped quickly inside and, closing the door behind him, slid into the priest's study.

"You are alone?"

Tommaso nodded. "Arnaldo is bringing the Englishman later. I thought that would be a safer way. Besides, I wanted to have a talk with you, Father Leone."

The priest waved him towards a chair.

"So the Englishman is here? He has a plan?"

"Yes, he has a plan."

"And more are coming here?"

"Two more are being dropped to-night. Two sergeants —one of them an American."

"Only three altogether? That would seem inadequate."

"For what is intended they will be sufficient."

Roberto broke in. "Assuredly they will be sufficient, and tanks and many troops will follow. More tanks and troops are following?"

Tommaso did not reply. His manner was subdued, almost sullen.

"We are saved," Roberto continued. "It is as I have said, we are saved. The brave British and our American cousins have a plan. They will save our so beautiful bridge. Do not doubt it. Father Leone here has been fearful and anxious, he has been worried, as is always the way with priests; but I say to him, 'Be reassured, all will be well. I, Roberto Conti, feel it in my bones.' "

"This Englishman—what sort of man is he?"

"Un capitano. He is determined, and has the gift of courage. Yes, there is no doubt that he is determined."

"Does he speak Italian?" Don Leone asked.

"He tells me that before the war he spent a holiday on Capri, and that he has also visited Santa Margherita and Portofino, and that during these holidays he picked up Italian. From the manner in which he speaks Italian, I believe him."

"It could be difficult."

"Senza dubbio. But you, Don Leone, speak English,

and so do I. Also Arnaldo is able to understand what is being said, and even Roberto understands a little. We shall manage sufficiently." Tommaso sighed, and stared gloomily at the floor. "Soon after the English captain arrived he told me his idea was to take lodgings in Fontana d'Amore; he seemed to think he could mingle unsuspected among our people. I explained to him, politely, that he was making an error."

"It seems strange that the British should have sent us a man who cannot speak Italian properly."

"He can speak it a little and, if one talks slowly, understands much of what is being said."

"Still, it is strange that the British should choose such a man."

"That, and some other things, is what worries me. I cannot help feeling that there has been some mistake, some muddle. The selection of this *capitano inglese* seems to have been done in a great hurry. When our message was received the British acted at once—and, in my opinion, without giving the matter the fullest consideration. For example, so great was the hurry that this *capitano* was not able to meet either of the two sergeants who are being dropped to-night; he knows nothing of their qualifications. As I said, the planning seems to have been done with great urgency—but without proper thought."

"It is disturbing."

"The *capitano inglese* had a long talk with me. He was frank and explained much. It seems that he came to Sicily with the 1st Airborne Division, who suffered affliction due to the pilots of the aircraft dropping them prematurely into the sea. In consequence these parachutists were collected by the British, and, as the *capi-*

tano said, 'put in a transit camp to reform.' This *Capitano* Kimber was one of these men, and he told me, 'I was sitting there without a job when this show of yours blew up, and I was hustled off to do it.' "

Roberto, who had been listening impatiently, broke in. "You are both seeing difficulties that do not exist," he said. "The anxiety has been too much for you. I am not surprised; you, Tommaso, have not experienced vexations and trials such as I, as Mayor of Fontana d'Amore, have. Day after day I was harassed by the Tedesci: 'Have you done this?' 'Do this at once!' 'Why was this not done?' I tell you, if I had allowed the strain to affect me I should have become like you. Have confidence, Tommaso, and you, Don Leone, have courage. We should now be rejoicing, drinking toasts in good wine, because our dear bridge is saved."

Tommaso looked at him sourly. "So?" he said. "Then let me tell you what the *capitano inglese* has come to do. He has come to blow up our bridge before the Tedesci do it."

For a moment there was complete silence.

"I do not understand you," said the priest at last.

"The Tedesci intend to blow up our bridge when most of their forces are safely across. The British intend to forestall them, to blow up our bridge before the Tedesci get across."

There was a pause, and then Tommaso added, "We now have two parties—instead of one—each determined to destroy our bridge."

Roberto leapt from his chair. "I do not believe you! It cannot be!" he cried. "I will not allow it! This beastly Britisher must be stopped."

"How?"

"How! How! Are you so spineless, Tommaso Ucelli, that you cannot deal with one single man? One man alone? Are there not such things as a knife in a man's throat? It would not be the first time you have done it, Tommaso Ucelli."

"That would be murder," the priest intervened. "I forbid such thoughts. Even the thought is a mortal sin."

Roberto snorted. "Then if you are so squeamish," he scoffed, "could he not be handed over to the Tedesci? Would it not be easy for some brave man to betray him?"

"And where would that get us?" asked Tommaso. "We would be where we started. The Tedesci would still be here to blow up our bridge when it suited them."

"Just a moment," Don Leone interposed, as Roberto was about to begin a heated reply. "If you, Tommaso, refused to help . . ."

"The *capitano inglese* and the two sergeants would do it themselves. Our help would be useful, but they could do it without us. Also, you must realize I am part of our organization, a military organization, and I have to obey my orders. When I learnt what the *capitano inglese* intended, and found he would not listen to reason, I got in touch with my superiors. I explained everything. They understood and were sympathetic, but they gave me orders—definite orders—to assist the *capitano inglese*. I was to obey him implicitly. They said they realized it was a great tragedy, a disaster for Fontana d'Amore, but the war must be viewed as a whole; it was necessary that the Germans should be trapped with their escape route destroyed. My orders were final."

"But if you . . ."

"Then I should be regarded by my Party as a traitor.

In a week or two men from Torino would come and shoot me in the back of my head. I have no wish that . . . And also I must think of my dear Francesca. Francesca would be greatly distressed if were shot in the back of the head. No, I must obey my orders. There is no other way."

"You are a coward, Tommaso Ucelli," stormed Roberto. "You should disregard your orders. Just because you think some Communists from Torino would come——"

Don Leone held up his hand. "Roberto, I pray you for a moment to be silent. I pray you will let me think. Tell me, Tommaso—do you believe this captain is serious, that nothing will cause him to change his mind?"

"I have told you he is determined. He is obstinate. I do not believe the good Stalin himself could change him. All to-day this *capitano inglese*, he has been studying the bridge, what he called 'getting the lie of the land.' He walked around continually and sat for long periods watching the Tedesci. It was most unwise, the danger was considerable, and I had to be with him."

As he finished speaking there came a faint tapping at the window.

"They are here," said Tommaso, "Arnaldo and the *capitano inglese*, they are here."

"I will let them in," said the priest. "And may God guide us all in what we say."

The Englishman was a tall man with fair, rather wavy hair, a knitted sweater covered the blouse of his battle-dress, giving an impression of untidiness. He smiled pleasantly at Don Leone and Roberto, and nodded cheerfully to Tommaso.

"Buon giorno. Come state," he said haltingly.

"Buona sera," grunted Tommaso.

Arnaldo followed the captain into the room and sat down, unsmiling, without saying a word.

"Well, I'm glad to meet every one. I suppose I'd better introduce myself—my name's Roy Kimber." The captain looked inquiringly at Tommaso. "I say, they do understand English, don't they? Difficult if we've got to work all the time in Italian, you know."

Tommaso nodded. "A little," he replied.

"I want to say we're very pleased that you tipped us off about what the Jerries were up to," said the captain. "Good show, we think."

Don Leone, who had been watching the Englishman closely ever since he had come into the room, sighed. Long and intimate experience of humanity had made the priest a sound judge of character. He was not deceived by the light manner of this *capitano inglese*. Tommaso had been right, this Roy Kimber was determined. It was going to be difficult to persuade him to change his mind; under that carefree attitude was real toughness, obstinacy.

"Let us all sit down," said the priest. Then, waiting until they were all seated, he began to speak in English.

Accustomed to presenting arguments in a way that would influence people, he spoke well and persuasively. With vivid touches he outlined the disaster the destruction of the bridge would bring to Fontana d'Amore, the calamity it would be, the bitter misery that would follow. He made clear the ruin that would come upon the countryside, the devastation that would turn it into an empty desert of bare rocks. He showed that the smashing of the bridge was not something like dropping bombs upon a town—towns could in time be rebuilt, life could start again; but here the flooding, the rushing torrents, would be the end of the precious soil, the extinction of the ground that had taken countless generations to create.

Tommaso listened closely, following every sentence, watching its effect upon the English captain. It seemed to Tommaso that the priest's words were impressing Roy Kimber, for he began to look embarrassed and to finger his collar. Clearly Kimber felt uncomfortable, and less sure of himself. Twice while Don Leone was speaking Roberto tried to interrupt, but the priest hushed him with a gesture, and Tommaso turned on him with such a threatening glare that Roberto stopped almost before he had begun.

Arnaldo said nothing.

"Yes, I do understand all that," said Roy Kimber at last, "and I am damned sorry—really I am. But we've got to do it. I know we'll do everything we can to help afterwards."

"There will be nothing that anyone can do afterwards," the priest said. "It will be irredeemable."

"I realize that now, and I'm . . . well, we have to do it. You see, it's this way : the Jerries have quite a big force holding out south of your river, and it's important for them to get this crowd back intact. They need them badly, to hold their new line up north. Now, if we destroy the bridge most of them won't get back. They'll have to stick it out where they are, and it will be most difficult for the Jerries to keep them properly supplied once the bridge has gone. We'll have 'em all in a corner with their trousers down."

"I do not think it reasonable," commented Arnaldo, "to expect all of them at the same time to have their trousers——"

"Is there no higher authority to whom we could explain?" interrupted the priest. "Surely, if your general realized the irreparable disaster that will follow he would find some other way?"

"I'm afraid," said Roy Kimber, "there is no other way. This bridge is the only way out or for bringing in supplies that the Jerries have for about fifteen miles. We've just got to keep this crowd where they are and cut their supply route. You see, where these Boche have slipped up is in not building some 'Bailey' bridges up and down the valley; they don't often overlook a thing like that, but I suppose they didn't think there was any hurry. It's come on them faster than they expected."

"But if you destroy our bridge you will be hampered when you have to cross the valley. Surely, it will be equally difficult for you?"

"We'll have to accept that. We may have to put up some 'Bailey' bridges, which will take time, of course, but between ourselves—I really oughtn't to say this— we'll probably be able to ignore this valley when we advance, attack at each end—sort of half-moon idea. Actually the whole scheme in blowing your bridge is to catch the Jerries who are now south of the valley. It's the chance of a lifetime."

"You are determined to bring this calamity on our people?"

"I don't want to. I'm sorry, really I am. I do see your point, but—well, I've been sent here to do it, and I can't back out now."

"When do you propose to do this?"

"To-night—well, early morning, anyway. I've already explained to Ucelli; two of our fellows are coming with the cable and the odds we need. They should be dropped at twenty-three hundred hours. Ucelli's crowd will bring them down here with the stuff. They should be here easily by one hundred hours. That gives us about four hours of darkness to get the lines fixed, and to touch it off."

Roberto could stand it no longer. "I will speak!" he cried. "You cannot keep hushing me. I demand to know what is being said. As Mayor of Fontana d'Amore, I have a right to be told. What have they been saying?"

Sullenly Tommaso told him. Roberto sprang from his chair and turned on Roy Kimber.

"You are a monster," he shouted quickly. "You are a beast. I will spit in your face. I have always hated the beastly British. You are worse than the Tedesci, far worse! You are a ruffian, a snake, a devil!"

Roberto's speech was so rapid that Kimber did not understand what was being shouted at him, but, realizing the man was upset, he smiled reassuringly. "Non vi capisco," he said, in what he believed was Italian. "I do not understand. Write it down, please."

"Briccone! Birbone! Scellerato! Assassino! Sporco bastardo!" stormed Roberto.

"Be silent!" cried Don Leone. "Roberto, be silent! Do you not see that he really does not understand a word you are shouting? And I thank God that he does not!"

Arnaldo nodded his head. "That he does not understand is clearly true," he agreed. "If he did we should have trouble here. But for once I agree with Roberto. What he says is accurate."

Don Leone took Roberto by the arm and pulled him back on to a chair. "I forbid you to use such words here, and to abuse the Englishman in this way," he said sternly.

"Can't you see it will do no good, that we will have to think of some other way to persuade him? Calm yourself, and be silent!"

"Will you tell him, please," said Kimber pleasantly, "I can't get what he is saying, he talks too quickly for me. I can see he's upset, and I believe it's about the bridge. Will you tell him I'm sorry, but the job just has to be done. I've been sent here specially to do it." Kimber glanced at his wrist-watch. "The other two should be safely down by now. We really ought to be getting off to meet them, as arranged."

"Tommaso Ucelli," said Roberto, "I demand that you cut this man's throat. Here and now, with Arnaldo to help you. As Mayor of Fontana d'Amore, I order you to do so."

"Don't you realize," said Tommaso sadly, "that I am a member of an organization, that I am acting under orders, and that if I disobey the results will be terrible. I am in anguish about the bridge as much as you are, but I have no alternative—none. Would you have me shot in the back of the head?"

"Willingly! Gladly! I would rejoice. It would be a good thing. You are a coward, Tommaso Ucelli; you are frightened for yourself. Some one has to stop this brutal Englishman. It is useless to expect Don Leone to act like a man, and if you will not do so I order Arnaldo here to act immediately."

"Then the men from Torino would shoot Arnaldo in the head."

Arnaldo nodded, and said, "I cannot accept such a possibility. I have your sister, Lisetta, to think about. I must—regretfully—do as I am ordered."

Kimber, who had been listening smilingly to the exchanges, turned to the priest and said politely, "I say, you speak English awfully well, you know."

With an effort Don Leone switched his mind from the anxieties and managed to reply to this social chit-chat. "I was for two years a curate in Birken'ead," he replied.

Kimber looked round at the gloomy faces around him. "You all look terribly depressed," he observed. "Of course I know that's natural, but it's no good taking it that way, is it? No good looking fed up. It's just one of those things that can't be helped."

"It always rains in Rome," muttered Tommaso.

"Always rains in Rome? I don't get you. I've been in Rome twice and it was jolly hot."

"Tommaso was quoting an old Tuscan proverb," explained Don Leone. "Rain makes people uncomfortable, so they look depressed. We in Tuscany feel the people in Rome always look despondent and melancholy. So when we see faces around us without joy we say, 'It always rains in Rome.' "

"In Rome," added Tommaso, "they are a cheerless lot."

The Englishman again glanced at his wrist-watch. "I really feel we ought to be going. I had a good look round to-day and I think I've got everything taped," he said, rising to his feet.

Don Leone made a last despairing appeal.

Roy Kimber was polite and sympathetic. Several times he repeated how sorry he was, but he made it quite clear that the destruction of the bridge was a necessity.

"Tommaso Ucelli, Arnaldo Vivarelli," said Roberto, "for the last time I order you to cut his throat."

Tommaso, except for a shrug of his shoulders, did not reply.

"It has been explained," said Arnaldo, "that it is not possible."

"Understand me," Don Leone said firmly, "every one of you—I will not have murder done here."

"I am not suggesting that it should be done here," protested Roberto indignantly, "in the house of a priest, adjoining the church. What I am asking is that he be taken to some convenient place——"

"What about getting along? The others will be waiting for us," said the potential victim, understanding scarcely a word of what had been said.

Tommaso grunted and rose to his feet.

Arnaldo also stood up.

"Un momento," said Don Leone. "While I could not allow murder, perhaps to restrain him, to hold him a prisoner until the danger is over——"

"I had thought of that," interrupted Tommaso, "but it would be worse than simply cutting his throat. When he was released he would have much to say, and then I should not only have our Party members seeking me, but also the British."

Roy Kimber smilingly found the priest's hand and shook it.

"I'm sorry about the bridge, but—well, it just has to be done. No other way—I'm sure you see that? Our people, when they get here, will do all they can to help, and we're most grateful for the way you tipped us off about what the Jerries are up to. Every one thought you'd all done a jolly good show."

Don Leone sank back in his chair.

"Well, let's get going," said Kimber, his hand on the doorknob. "Buon giorno, and—grazie. Yes, indeed—molte grazie."

The three men clumped out of the room and closed the door behind them.

"They have gone to bring ruin upon my people," said Don Leone. "The misery that will follow . . ."

Roberto stared at him in silence. For once he was speechless.

5

The Bridge

ON LEAVING THE PRESBYTERY KIMBER, TOMMASO, and Arnaldo crept cautiously across the square and then along a narrow street which led them gradually to open country. They trod as silently as possible, keeping in the shadows, and stopping from time to time to listen for any sound of approaching footsteps. As Tommaso whispered, you never knew when the Tedesci had patrols watching the roads.

The moon had not yet risen, but the cloudless bowl of the sky sprinkled with the white dots of stars seemed to provide a haze of light, so that the grey track of the lane was easy to follow. After about ten minutes walking they reached a pine-wood, and, passing along the edge of this for a little way, came to a narrow path leading into the trees.

Tommaso turned up the path into the darkness, but about five yards farther on he stopped. "We must wait here a little," he whispered, "and listen. We may be being followed. Listen most carefully."

For what seemed an age, they stood silent. In the stillness even the rustle of their own clothes and the sound of their own breathing were audible.

At last Tommaso whispered again. "I think it is all right. Come quietly."

Their eyes now accustomed to the leafy darkness, they followed the path for a few minutes, and then, at a place where it took a sharp bend and the ground rose higher on one side, Tommaso pushed his way, scrambling upward, into the bracken.

"We wait for the others here," he said softly.

"Gosh, what I'd give for a cigarette," said Kimber.

Arnaldo rustled farther down into the bracken. "It would be highly dangerous," he whispered.

Overhead the branches of the pine-trees, touching each other, made a faint rippling sound, a gentle *Ssh-ssh*. In silence the three men waited.

From time to time Kimber peered at the fingers of his wrist-watch. "Gets on your nerves, this waiting, doesn't it? Sort of tension. I wish they'd come. They ought to have been here before now." He fidgeted.

"They will come," murmured Tommaso. "We are about an hour's walk from where they were to be dropped. It is not to be expected——"

"Sure we're at the right spot?"

Tommaso did not reply, but Arnaldo muttered "Senza dubbio," and added, "What I fail to comprehend fully is why the British did not send an aircraft—a bomber—and blow the bridge up that way."

"A bridge is a difficult target to hit. Look how the Jerries tried to do it in London and how nearly every bridge across the Thames was left standing. We've rather given up the idea of using bombers for bridges."

A quarter of an hour later Kimber spoke again. "They're late," he whispered. "They should have been here by now. What's worrying me is the moon—it's getting up, and that isn't going to make it any easier for us."

"If your aircraft was exact and dropped them at twenty-three hundred hours as arranged," Tommaso reasoned, "they would have to be located, and the materials they had brought collected. Burdened with cables and charges, it would take them some time to get here. It is, as I said, an hour's walk."

"Also," said Arnaldo, "a man who has just been leaping out of an aircraft and floating about the sky on a dark night is probably not at his best for a little while. He may not feel inclined to walk briskly."

Kimber grunted.

Five minutes later Tommaso sat up suddenly. "They are here!" he whispered. "Some people are coming up the path. Listen!"

"Do not move," said Arnaldo. "It may be a Tedesci patrol."

"I am not a fool," Tommaso retorted. "If it is the Tedesci, they will go straight on up the path—we hope —but if it is our people they will turn off into the bracken."

It was not a German patrol. Soon two men left the path and began scrambling upward into the bracken.

Tommaso stood up. "Giovanni?"

"Tommaso," came the reply. "Yes, I am here."

"This is Giovanni Marrini," said Tommaso, turning to Kimber. "He is a good man."

Giovanni Marrini bowed. "To meet you, *capitano*, is a pleasure. I am at your service."

"Are there only two of you?" asked Kimber.

"Yes, only two. I deeply regret to tell you the English sergeant, poor fellow, suffered an injury when he reached the ground. He landed in a tree, and, while endeavouring to extract himself, fell to the earth."

"Killed?"

"By no means—a broken leg, assuredly, and perhaps some other minor distresses. We could not be quite sure because he was impatient when we examined him. He was somewhat annoyed."

"That was to be expected," commented Arnaldo.

"What have you done with him?" asked Tommaso.

"Be assured no traces have been left. We carried him to the cottage above Clemente. The Morelli family have him in their care, and to-morrow they will bring a doctor to him. The Englishman is hidden above the Morelli's stable—on a most comfortable bed of straw."

Kimber peered into the darkness. "And you're the American sergeant?" he asked. "You got down all right?"

"You betcha," said the man indifferently. "Bob Tuttle, of Great Neck, New Jersey."

"You know we've got to blow up a bridge? I don't understand much about explosives myself—not my line —but I suppose you are an expert?"

The American laughed, and Tommaso said "Hush."

"Back home I was a salesman—textiles; yes, sir, textiles. Since I've been in the forces my job's been trucks. I know about most things, but explosives—no, sir, I despise explosives."

To Kimber, the situation began to seem a little difficult. He had a rough idea of how explosive charges worked, and a vague idea of the correct procedure when handling them, but he foresaw problems arising, and possibly unpleasant results.

"I suppose the English sergeant was the explosive expert. We haven't much time, but if we get in a jam perhaps he could explain things."

The American chuckled. "Say, he don't know nuthin'. Since he's been in your outfit, I gather, he's been drivin' some general around. Before that, I guess he was workin' as a butler, for a duke."

"Look here," said Kimber. "One of you must know something about explosives—you or the other sergeant; if not why did they send you?"

"Jest because I speak the lingo, I guess. My Mom was Italian, and as a kid I was raised in an Italian section. Yes, sir, that's the only reason I can think of why they picked on me—except, maybe, because I didn't get on with my captain. He was a guy from La Grange, Georgia; narrow-minded about dames; sorta puritanical; a real goody-good. He's been tryin' to have me posted ever since I joined his outfit. Maybe he figured this was his chance to kiss me good-bye."

"Well," said Kimber, after a pause, "anyway, you brought the charges and things?"

"Sure, we brought 'em."

Giovanni intervened. "Assuredly, we have here with us everything," he said. "Two drums of electric cable, a large switch, and—see—these three canisters."

"I consider it may be unwise to wave them about like that," remarked Arnaldo. "They should, I feel, be treated with respect."

Kimber took the orange-coloured canisters from Giovanni, examined them, and wished he could remember more about what had been said at that lecture—the one he had attended that had dealt with the subject of explosives.

At the top of each tin there were two terminals, clearly marked: one terminal +, the other −. A label attached to each tin seemed to give some instructions, or possibly only a warning.

Kimber peered at the labels, trying to read the wording, and wished that he had a light. "I don't think it's going to be too difficult," he said at last. "I think you put one end of the cable—it's double flex—to each of the terminals on the canister, and the other end to the terminals on a battery, with the switch in between. It says a twelve-volt battery."

"I recollect that the guy who saw us off did mention sumthin' about a battery. Yeah, he said an ordinary automobile battery was what was needed."

"They didn't send one?"

"Nope. I guess they reckoned there'd be plenty of automobile batteries around here."

Kimber turned to Tommaso. "Can you get a car battery, twelve volts?" he inquired.

Tommaso said he could; there was a garage on the outskirts of the town that was kept by an honest man. The best thing would be for Giovanni to go there, wake up the proprietor, and bring the battery to the bridge. To do it that way would be safer than the whole party going and would also save time. "While he is collecting the battery," said Tommaso, "we can be going direct to the bridge."

Giovanni was given his instructions and told where and how to rejoin the party at the bridge. And then, allowing Giovanni a few minutes start—for as Arnaldo said, "Four men move more silently than five"—Kimber and the others crawled back on to the path. Walking cautiously, stopping at intervals to listen, they went across the main road and along narrow tracks winding among the little farmsteads. In single file, carrying the cables and canisters between them, Tommaso leading, Arnaldo at the rear, they trudged on. Kimber realized Tommaso was guiding them round the outskirts of the town towards the river.

No one spoke except the American, who once or twice

whispered to Tommaso an inquiry—something about "the dames around here": a question that Tommaso, considering both the subject and the present time unsuitable, ignored.

Kimber was beginning to worry seriously about the shortage of time. It was now almost two o'clock, and in another three hours it would be getting light. Three hours —barely sufficient time to place the canisters and lay out the cable, for these were jobs that would have to be done silently and unseen. And the moon had now come up. This would give light and would make things more difficult. Knowing the Germans, Kimber realized the bridge would be well guarded, the sentries alert and watchful. To crawl over the loose rubble, the stones beside the river, to fix the canisters against the main pillar, and place the cable without being seen, would not be easy.

"I made a good recce," he whispered to the American, when the party paused for a few moments. "I think, Sergeant . . ."

"Call me Bob," murmured the other. "An' say, I been figurin' out why they posted me to this set-up. I guess it must ha' been 'cause that captain wanted to lose me. He was a guy with no natural feelin' about dames, jest no understandin'. Yes, sir, he an' I had trouble at most every town where we stopped."

Tommaso said, "Hush."

"Lemme tell you a story 'bout . . ."

Kimber continued to worry about lack of time and the increasing light from the moon. They began to walk forward again, and at long last came to a path, running parallel to the river, near to the bridge.

Tommaso stopped. "It is unwise to go nearer. It is

here that I told Giovanni to bring the battery," he told
them.

Kimber crouched down. "Now this is my plan," he
said. "Two of the canisters—all three if I can manage
it—will be put up against that arch, the tall, thin arch
on the left. I suppose the canisters should be fastened to
the stonework and heavy boulders be put against them
to make the blast more effective. But it's impossible to
go knocking spikes into the arches—even if we had the
spikes—or to go rolling boulders about; so we'll just have
to hope for the best. I'll lay the cable out at the same
time as I take out the canisters—one journey, trailing the
cable behind me as I creep forward. You can tie the
charges with string round my waist, so as to leave my
hands free to carry the cable and pay it out. When the
canisters are in place I connect the cable ends to those
two terminals and creep back, then when I'm back again
we connect to the battery and switch on."

"I do not agree," said Tommaso sullenly.

"Am I in charge or are you?" demanded Kimber.

Tommaso shrugged his shoulders. "I have no wish to
do this destruction," he muttered, "to do an act that
will destroy my town and bring unhappiness and misery
is detestable. Arnaldo and I will be hated for ever."

"That is very true," commented Arnaldo.

"But," Tommaso went on, "I have had my orders, and
with the greatest reluctance I obey them. It is I, not you,
capitano, who will crawl out and place the charges. You
are not fit for such work."

"What do you mean? It is my job and I'm going——"

"I say you are not fit because you are—forgive me,
I wish to be courteous—like a clumsy horse. Look how
you have crashed and stumbled on this night's walk!

Enough noise to wake the dead ones! Why, if you were to attempt to cross those stones and erect the charges you would have every Tedesci shouting and shooting at you. Why, you would never get half-way."

"He is accurate," said Arnaldo. "Experience in the mountains has taught Tommaso to move silently and without being seen. You are, as he says so truthfully, like a clumsy horse—or an elephant."

"I am going——" began Kimber.

"You are not, and I will tell you why. I will tell you another reason that will settle the matter. The Tedesci have machine-guns—seven of them—on that bridge. If they do hear anything they will carpet the ground with bullets, and anyone on the stones will be hit, not once, but many times. Once the firing starts, it is only a body that will be found afterwards. Now if I, an Italian known to be a partisan, am found dead, that will be accepted; but if an Englishman, a British soldier, were found, that would be serious. They would know you had been dropped by parachute, they would guess there might be others. There would be searches, yes—every house would be searched, also the woods and the farms. Arms and other things would be found. The Tedesci would burn down homes, take hostages, torture them until they said all they knew. There would be people shot, and our whole organization round here would be destroyed. I cannot accept such a calamity."

"He is right, *capitano*," said Arnaldo. "If you try it is a certainty a body will be found and much disaster will follow. If he tries there is at least a chance, and if he fails far less trouble will occur."

The American, who had been listening impatiently, spoke. "Do you want me to git out there an' have a crack?" he drawled. "Is that what you guys are tryin' to say?"

"No, most certainly," replied Arnaldo. "It is well known that the Americans have no delicacy. I do not mean to be impolite when I tell you that if the *capitano inglese* is like an elephant you are like a Brontosaurus."

"Is that so! Now listen, Rigoletto, lemme tell you . . ."

Kimber tried to argue with Tommaso. It was clear that here military discipline did not exist and that a direct order was useless. Tommaso was obstinate, his mind made up.

"I disagree that the bridge should be blown up, I am fully in agreement with what Roberto said about that, but my organization has given me orders to assist you, and so whatever my feelings, I must do so. You are incapable of placing those charges and the cable without being discovered, and for a dead Englishman to be found here would bring much trouble, therefore, as I said, it is I who will go."

"We are wasting our time," Arnaldo said urgently. "In less than two hours it will be light, then no one can go—which in my opinion would be an excellent thing. But all this talk is getting us nowhere. Troppo parlare."

Kimber turned suddenly. "Some one is coming!" he exclaimed.

The sound of cautious footsteps was unmistakable, then two figures keeping in the shadows could be seen.

"Giovanni," Arnaldo explained calmly.

Giovanni, with another man, carrying a black car battery between them, stepped silently among the party. He bent close to Kimber and indicated the stranger was the proprietor of the garage, who had provided the battery.

"Here, tie these charges round my waist," said Tommaso roughly.

"I order you . . ." began Kimber as Arnaldo, producing a length of cord from his pocket, stepped forward and started tying.

Tommaso turned his head. "I am going, not you," he said. "I am an Italian in my own country, and if this beastly thing is to be done I will do it. If you try to stop me I swear I will fire my pistol in the air, I will shout, I will warn the Tedesci. Understand me—although I hate it, I am going, not you."

"You will obey me."

"I will not. It is for me to go."

"You see," said Arnaldo placidly, "he has the gift of courage."

"You are a liar, Arnaldo," Tommaso snapped, "for I am very, very frightened."

Arnaldo went on binding the charges. When all was ready Tommaso took the end of the cable in one hand and tied it firmly to his wrist. "Pay it out gently," he instructed. "As I creep forward I mean to leave it loose behind me. Keep the drum turning freely."

"Don't forget—red wire to positive, black to negative," Kimber, who had given up the argument, urged. "And . . . I say . . . well, good luck."

"Jest plumb crazy," remarked the American.

Tommaso did not reply. Softly he walked to the edge of the path, then, lowering himself gently so that he lay flat upon the ground, he began to move, sliding, wriggling away from them down towards the river.

Lying flat, their heads over the edge of the path, the five men watched him, Kimber and Arnaldo paying out the soft cable from the drum behind them. The moon was not as bright as it had been, and there were banks of clouds in the sky now, so that when these obscured the moon there came long periods when the river-bank was almost in darkness. Tommaso was taking advantage of this cover, stopping and lying still when the ground was lighted, moving forward only when the clouds darkened the landscape. The river running swiftly and splashing noisily against large boulders in midstream drowned any sound of Tommaso's descent, and Kimber began to have a hope—a hope that somehow he dare not allow himself to believe in—that the charges would be put in place and Tommaso would get back safely.

They lost sight of Tommaso after a time, and only the gradual drawing out of the cable told them that he was still moving away from them. They could see clearly the sentries and the machine-guns on the bridge. There appeared to be four sentries stationed at intervals, and from time to time these marched briskly to and fro. Obviously there was no slackness in the way the bridge was guarded, the sentries were alert and watching, the way in which one of them would pause occasionally and, leaning over the parapet, stare down towards the river, made Kimber feel as if he were swallowing a golf-ball.

Suddenly Arnaldo spoke.

"I see him again! He is there by that large rock—look, near that patch of grey stones."

Kimber and the others stared intently, but none of them except Arnaldo was sure that he could see Tommaso.

"If he's reached that rock he's almost at the bridge," said Kimber. "He may manage it yet, but time's getting short. Oh, blast that moon!"

They lay, peering across the grey rocky bank below

them, watching the dark outline of the bridge, the sentries with their ready rifles. Lying there waiting, the suspense made Kimber feel that he wanted to vomit.

At last the cable ceased to move. They remained tense, not daring to hope, expecting the cable to start drawing away from them again, as it had done dozens of times in the last half-hour; but this time the cable remained still. When there had been no movement for nearly ten minutes Arnaldo spoke.

"He's got there," he said. "Now we wait to see if he returns intact."

"Yeah," muttered Bob. "Yeah, I guess he's made it an' is fixin' those charges. I guess it's jest as well, because that cable's pretty nearly all out."

It was almost half an hour later when they saw the dark smudge of a man's body creeping towards them across the rocks. Slowly, yard by yard, Tommaso moved up the bank. Kimber felt that last hundred yards, that last ten minutes, was the worst to bear of the whole journey.

Then, at last, Tommaso was within reach, and, gripping two of their outstretched hands, pulled himself up beside them.

"Good show," said Kimber inadequately, "good show." It was all that he could think of to say. He was wondering what the others would think of him if he were to crawl away and be sick.

"I have fixed the two wires correctly," Tommaso said. "All three charges are beside the arch; I could not attach them to the stonework, that was impossible. I have doubts that the charges placed as they are will be sufficient for their purpose."

"I think they will," said Kimber. "The Jerries must

have put a lot of explosive round the bridge, and what I hope is that our tins will set the Jerries' stuff off."

"Speriamo," said Arnaldo. "But what puzzles me is why the British did not send us some kind of time charges —something which one could set to explode after one was safely away."

"Say, these Limeys, they jest don't use their grey matter. Lemme tell you 'bout——"

"The battery," said Kimber, ignoring the slur; "we'd better get it coupled up."

Arnaldo nodded. "That is good sense," he replied. "It is to be hoped that all works satisfactorily."

Tommaso grunted. "Let us get this horrible thing over quickly."

Kimber moved close to him. "I'm sorry you've been dragged into this, Tommaso. I know how you feel about it, and—well, I'm sorry. It was a good show, you going like that, but I wish I could have stopped you. It was my job, not yours."

"He had no option," said Arnaldo cheerfully. "The organization had given him orders to assist. If you had gone you would have been seen and shot, and that would have brought much trouble upon us from the Tedesci, and the organization would have been annoyed."

Giovanni brought the battery to the end of the cable, and Kimber began attaching the wires—one to the battery, the other to the switch, then a short length from the switch to the other terminal on the battery. With a pair of pliers, he went over each connexion, tightening them.

"All O.K.," he said at last. "Now every one lie down flat. We don't know what the blast will be like."

Without saying a word, the four Italians moved back

behind Kimber and lay down. But Tuttle did not lie down. As a compromise, he knelt.

"I wanna git a good view," he explained.

Kimber put his hand on the switch. "Ready. One, two, three." He pressed the plunger. Nothing happened. He pressed the plunger again harder. "One of the wires not making contact." He tried to tighten the terminals still more with a pair of pliers. "Seem firm," he said doubtfully. "Wish I knew more about this job." Then, as another thought occurred to him, he bent towards Tommaso. "You're quite certain you wired up properly on the charges?"

"That is certain. Positive. I am not a fool."

Twice more Kimber pressed the plunger. "Something wrong," he said unnecessarily.

"Here, let me have a try," said Tommaso. He jerked the plunger up and down several times.

"If I may speak," said Giovanni, who had been having a conversation in a low voice with the garage proprietor. "Our friend here, who is of course an expert on such things, believes he knows what is the trouble."

"Then for God's sake let him come and put it right."

The garage proprietor came forward. "In my opinion," he said, "the failure is because the battery is a new one and requires charging. To obtain results, signore, it would seem that current is desirable, and as yet, of course, there is no current in the battery."

Tommaso turned on him like a springing tiger, but the man cut him short.

"Signore Ucelli, it is not courteous to talk to me in that way. I am not to blame. Giovanni here, he comes and demands from me a battery. He says it must be a good one, so I get him the best I have—one unused. I did not know for what purpose you wanted it, or when you wanted to use it. I was not told. It is not my fault that the battery is as yet uncharged."

"But you saw Tommaso go out there to the bridge," said Kimber, "risking his life. Why didn't you speak before he went?"

"Ah, signore, I was so impressed with his bravery, and so worried for my own safety—I, here alone at night, among desperate men, and within reach of the Tedesci. Thought of such things as batteries was not in my mind."

With vivid words Tommaso expressed his feelings. Arnaldo nodded his agreement. Only Bob seemed to remain unmoved.

"Nutty," he remarked, spitting contemptuously. "Yes, sir, nutty—plumb ca-razy."

"How long will it take you to get another battery?" demanded Kimber.

"I have no other battery," said the garage proprietor. "You will appreciate, signore, that with this terrible war upon us, cars are not being used. I, Enrico Amaro, have had to give up my business, and I now work as a hairdresser. All the batteries I have are, as we say, 'flat'— empty, uncharged."

"Can't we get one out of some car or lorry?"

"Signore, there are no cars or trucks except those controlled by the military. I would remind you, signore, with respect, that here in Italy we are at war."

Arnaldo, who had been trying to hush Tommaso, turned and joined in the conversation. "What he says is true," he stated. "It is impossible to obtain a battery fresh and eager for work. What will have to be done is to ask this good man to take this battery back to his home and charge it fully."

"Can you do that?"

"Senza dubbio," said Enrico. "A twenty-four-hour charge will undoubtedly make a big difference. By this time to-morrow, signore, you can have a battery of the finest."

Kimber took Tommaso aside and asked him was there no way to surmount the difficulty. Another twenty-four-hours delay was serious, as the destruction of the bridge was urgent and immediate. Could nothing be done?

"I know of no way," Tommaso said sullenly. "I do not wish to talk about any of this matter. I am what the British call 'fed up'!"

Kimber thought over the whole situation quickly. It really seemed that the earliest a battery could be obtained would be the following night. Why the hell had they sent the kind of charges that required batteries and cables? There were, he knew, several types of charges that explored on a time fuse; why had they sent this clumsy outfit? No good getting worked up. He would have to manage with the stuff they had sent him, and as no battery was obtainable, he would have to wait until to-morrow night. He would have to leave it. There was no other way. Not his fault, he had done all he could. Blast them! Sending him, when he knew nothing about explosives, and sending the sergeants, who knew even less. The whole affair was a scandal, did no one use their brains? Anyway, the moon was going down now, but it would be daylight in another hour. Those charges and the cable could not be left where they were. Those bright orange tins—why must they paint them orange?—would be seen easily when the sun came up. And some Jerry might go down to the river and trip over the cable. No, somehow the tins and the cables had to be brought back. He could not let them stay there as a warning to the Jerries. Besides, he needed the things for to-morrow night.

Tommaso, who had also been considering the position, started to speak. "We haven't much time," he reminded them; "in about an hour it will be light."

"By which time," commented Arnaldo, "it would be advisable for us all to be in our homes."

"The less people about here, the better," Tommaso agreed. "It has been proved often that it is not wise to have more together than is strictly necessary. Giovanni and Enrico had better leave us immediately, taking the battery with them and putting it on charge. The American must also go with them." Tommaso turned to Giovanni. "When you have seen the battery and Enrico safely home you will take the American and find him a safe lodging in the town. I do not want him hiding with us in the hills."

"What's the big idea? Lemme tell you, when it comes to hidin' you don't know nuthin'. Why, once in Atlanta I had a dame's two brothers *and* her pop *and* her mom trailin' me with guns for a week."

"I have already got the *capitano inglese* and a British sergeant with a broken leg on my hands; is that not enough? You will be safe in the town, you speak Italian as we do, and if you can behave with sense it is safer that you should be in the town until you are wanted."

"I cannot see why he should ever be wanted," remarked Arnaldo. "I cannot see what use he will ever be. Do not bolt your door with a boiled carrot."

"Say, now listen——"

"When you, Giovanni," ordered Tommaso, "have

placed the American in some discreet house, you will return to the hills. It may be that some messages have come in during the night. If so, bring them to me. I will be at the Hermitage, and the *capitano inglese* will be with me. You understand? Enrico and the battery to their home, the American to a lodging in the town, back to the hills, and then bring me any messages to the Hermitage. Is that clear?"

"It is clear to me—it is also clear to me that when I see you again I may be somewhat tired."

Kimber listened to the instructions Tommaso gave and nodded approval; they suited his own plans well. A few minutes later the three men set off, Giovanni and Enrico holding the battery between them, Bob Tuttle spitting contemptuously. As they disappeared into the darkness, Kimber moved to the edge of the path, then quickly, before the others could stop him, he lowered himself down on to the stones below and began crawling towards the river.

"It's no good you arguing," he said as Tommaso started to follow him, obviously with the intention of pulling Kimber back. "I am going this time—not you. You aren't going twice."

Tommaso began to protest.

"Shut up!" said Kimber. "It's dark now, and I shall manage it all right. So get back and shut up!"

He started wriggling swiftly away down the bank.

Tommaso hesitated, then, with a gesture of exasperation, climbed back on to the path. "He is," he said bitterly to Arnaldo, "what the British call a fool of blood."

6

The Trouble

IT WAS ONE OF THOSE PERFECT MORNINGS THAT COME to Italy in autumn. A cloudless, transparent sky of deep blue, a gentle breeze and soft sunshine that gave promise of a good day to come. Although in the valley some traces of white mist still lingered, the air up on the hillside was crystal clear. The edges of the distant mountain-tops showed pearly grey against the blue of the sky, and then lower down the mountain-sides were the dark belts of pines, and below these the grey lines of olive-trees, with the vivid green alfalfa growing beneath them. Occasionally the glitter of water from tumbling streams flickered among the greenery.

At a small farmstead farther down the track two white oxen drawing a plough behind them were moving majestically to the start of a long day's work.

Trudging up the mountain path, with Tommaso just ahead of him, leading the way, Kimber thought that on a day like this it was good to be alive. "Pity I didn't get those three canisters," he said.

Tommaso looked back over his shoulder. "If, as you say, you covered them well with stones," he answered, "it is most unlikely that they will be noticed. There is no need for concern."

"I just couldn't manage to tie them round my waist, and I couldn't climb back carrying them in my hands. As it was, I was making a noise and was going to give the game away."

"Be assured you behaved wisely. They are well hidden beneath the stones and will be there in the place we want them when we go again to-night. It was getting the cable away that really mattered; the cable could easily have been seen, and if it had been seen it would have warned the Tedesci."

"Yes, I'm glad we got that back," said Kimber. "Gosh, I'm tired!"

Tommaso nodded. "That is to be expected," he replied sympathetically. "I also do not feel alert, and in addition I am hungry. But now we have not far to go."

On they trudged. Below in the valley wraiths of blue mist from wood-fires were rising from the farmsteads. From a monastery, perched on the hillside a little way below them, came the sound of a bell ringing in the campanile—not a dismal tolling, nor a raucous clanging, of metal, but a cheerful, mellow sound that seemed to be summoning them back again, proclaiming that there, within those ancient walls, they would find quietude and peace.

The path curved round a heap of large rocks, and here Tommaso stopped, listened for perhaps a minute, and stared intently out over the countryside; then, crouching down, he crawled into the bracken, and Kimber followed him. Pushing carefully forward, endeavouring to leave no tracks by crushing down the tall ferns, they reached at last a low stone building, old and dilapidated, almost completely hidden by the vegetation.

"Long ago," explained Tommaso, "this was the home of a hermit. Members of my organization use it now, but only in the daytime, for at night it is haunted by a ghost."

They went inside. The Hermitage consisted of only one room. In one corner was a pile of dry bracken and a few blankets. Beside these was a wooden box in which were two or three plates, a few forks, some tins, and a "Thermos" flask. Tommaso explained that it would be unwise to make a fire—as he put it, "Smoke is a big telltale"—but foreseeing that they might have to use the Hermitage this morning, he had arranged for the "Thermos" flask to be filled with hot coffee. He poured some of the steaming coffee into two cups and handed one to Kimber, then, opening one of the larger tins, he produced some crisp rolls, butter, a jar of marmalade, and two bars of chocolate. It seemed to Kimber, as he drank and munched, that food and drink had never tasted so good.

When they had finished eating Tommaso explained that Kimber must wrap himself in the blankets and lie down upon the bracken in the corner. "It is necessary that we both have sleep so that we may be untired for the work to-night," he told Kimber; "but we may not both sleep at the same time. One of us must keep watch, so we will take it in turns. I will wake you in three hours."

After a brief protest as to why he should have first sleep Kimber rolled himself in the blankets and settled down.

Tommaso sat down, his back against the doorpost. "More than once those of our organization who have not kept proper watch have been surprised by the Tedesci and even sometimes by the Carabinieri," he continued. "When they did waken it was too late to get away. A dear friend of mine, Alfredo Trani, was caught, owing to keeping an improper watch. They shot him three days later, at Arezzo."

Kimber closed his eyes, and soon he was in a deep sleep.

Tommaso sat watching and listening. He began to think over the events of the past night: perhaps it was a good thing that battery had not been charged, though it was certainly true, the *capitano* would undoubtedly try again to-night, and that even if he failed again the Tedesci would blow up the bridge when they were ready to leave. Yes, it did seem that the calamity was certain to come, sooner or later. But until the bridge was actually destroyed, there was always a chance that something might arise to prevent the catastrophe. *Domani.* There was wisdom— and possibly hope—in *domani.* The British were strange people. You never knew what they would do next, they were so casual and had a way of muddling things. Of course he rather liked that *capitano.* The *capitano* re- minded him of a child playing a game. But that Ameri- can sergeant—ah, Tommaso was not sure about that one! Perhaps it had been unwise to find the American a lodging in the town. He seemed to think too much about women; it would be well to watch him closely. Tommaso had a sincere respect for women, and some of the American's remarks had been distasteful to him. No, Tommaso would not trust that American out of sight with a nice girl.

Kimber opened his eyes, suddenly roused by a feeling that something was pressing hard on his mouth. Now fully awake, he found his head being forced backward by the pressure of Tommaso's left hand on his lips.

"Zitto!" Tommaso whispered. "There is some one on the path above. I think there is only one person, so it may be Giovanni, but do not speak until we are sure."

Kimber sat up.

"Yes, it is Giovanni," said Tommaso at last. "He is creeping cautiously through the bracken."

A minute or two later Giovanni, holding a basket, stood at the door of the hut. "Buon giorno," he said cheerfully, putting the basket down. "I have brought a flask of wine, some cheese, and some fresh rolls."

Tommaso did not reply; Kimber said, "Thanks a lot."

"I have also brought a message," Giovanni went on, "a message that may displease you both. It came through the radio early this morning. It has been decoded. See, I have it here."

He fumbled in his pocket and produced a piece of grey paper.

"Give it to me," said Tommaso, taking the paper. He read it slowly, then, without a word, tossed it angrily to Kimber.

Kimber began to read, then stared at the message in amazement.

"Oh, hell!" he exclaimed.

The message ran:

Most secret memorize only destroy immediately stop due error canisters sent you signal flares stop not repeat not explosives stop correct materials being dropped tonight stop place and time notified figures twenty two hundred hours message ends.

Evening had come, and Roberto, lying upstairs on his bed, was wakened by the sound of raised voices—angry voices that echoed through the priest's house.

Are they mad? said Roberto to himself, springing up. Do they want to bring the Tedesci here? Do they not realize what could happen to me if the Tedesci came?

He trotted out of his bedroom, across the little landing, and began to go down the stairs. Half-way down he stopped. Was it wise for him to venture any farther? Who was there below, in Don Leone's room? He recognized the voice of Tommaso shouting—yes, shouting. It was clear that Tommaso was very angry indeed. He seemed to be threatening some one. Roberto caught the words *I will cut his throat!* The voices of Don Leone and Arnaldo, apparently trying to soothe and remonstrate at one and the same time, could be heard, and even they were not speaking quietly. Once Roberto caught the sound of the *capitano inglese* saying something about, "Now look here . . . look here . . ." It was clear that below in the priest's room a first-class row was in progress. The voice of Tommaso came again distinctly. "I will not be calm! This is no time to be calm! I tell you I will cut him into little pieces!"

Roberto tiptoed back again. Then, like a child who listens to a ghost story although he knows it will frighten him, Roberto leant over the banisters. Among the babble of voices he heard that of Maria. So Maria too was in this argument, was she? "For shame, Tommaso Ucelli, it is a wonder that the holy saints do not strike you dead!" she was shouting. "I tell you, Father Leone knows nothing about it. Poor soul, he has been away since early morning." "I am not concerned about Don Leone," thundered Tommaso, "but when I catch that creature, that snake, I will crush him until the blood runs out."

Roberto stood trembling. He had no reason, he told himself, to think that Tommaso was referring to him, but a conscience that over the years had developed a habit of feeling guilty suggested he, Roberto, might be in danger.

"Wait until I get at him," Tommaso was barking. "Just wait until I catch him."

Roberto retreated hurriedly into his bedroom and closed the door. Bitterly he realized there was no key. He scuttled over to the window and—leaning out—tried to decide if it would be possible, if the worst came to the worst, to reach that water-spout. No, even if he did reach it the pipe looked unsafe, and even if it would support his weight he knew he would never be able to hold on.

The sound of some one coming upstairs sent Roberto pressing backward, in panic, hard against the wardrobe.

The bedroom door opened.

"You had better come downstairs," said Don Leone.

"I will do no such thing," Roberto replied, his voice quavering, but firm in his intention. "It would be madness."

"Tommaso says if you do not come down he will come up here."

"The sheets off the bed—quick, we could make a rope of them! Quick, Father Leone, help me! He will kill me, you do not want murder in your house."

The priest shook his head. "It is not you Tommaso is threatening," he said. "He only wants to hear what you can tell him."

"You are sure? Father Leone, you are sure?"

"Oh, come downstairs," said the priest irritably. "I insist you come downstairs."

Don Leone leading, Roberto, ready for rapid retreat if this should prove necessary, followed doubtfully behind. As they descended the stairs, the voice of Maria came to them.

"It is what I have said from the first. A great fat Fascist, a godless Communist, and an English heretic in the house of a saintly priest. What could be expected but trouble?

The Holy Pope would tell you the same. If I had my way they would be swept out now into the street!"

Don Leone reached the sitting-room door and, pulling the reluctant Roberto after him, went into the room.

"Imbecille!" Tommaso greeted Roberto. "Why did you do it?"

Roberto stood white and speechless.

The priest intervened. "Let me tell Roberto what we have been talking about," he said. "Let me speak. This morning after early Mass I went away to say another Mass, at Paterna; I remained there visiting people all day. Soon after I left here Giovanni Marrini arrived, bringing with him an American, and asked——"

"Asked!" interrupted Maria. "I tell you, demanded would be more accurate—demanded that this American should be given lodging. Lodging! As if this was not the house of a priest of God but a hotel!"

"While Giovanni was discussing the matter——"

"There was no discussion. I just told him Don Leone was not here and told him to be off and take his American with him. Is it likely that I would have an American in this house, even if it were not already overrun with Fascists and Communists? I said, 'Be off with both of you.'"

"Then," continued Don Leone, "while Maria was speaking to Giovanni, you, Roberto, came downstairs from your bedroom. What we all want to know is what happened after that?"

"Nothing," said Roberto, a firm believer in the stout denial. "Nothing whatever."

"I will have the truth," stormed Tommaso. "You went out with the American. What happened? Tell me before I lose control of myself and slit your throat!" He moved closer to the trembling Roberto, who saw with alarm that Tommaso was holding an unsheathed knife.

Roberto spoke quickly. "Giovanni explained to me that he needed a lodging for this American," he babbled. "It was clear that without the support of Don Leone I could not persuade Maria to provide accommodation here. Being an unhappy fugitive myself, I felt sympathy for this American cousin, and I decided, at whatever risk to myself, I would assist him. So I told Giovanni, who was in a hurry and anxious to get away, to leave the American to me. At the danger of my life, I would take him into the town and find him a place of safety."

"You were not in any danger," commented Arnaldo. "At eight hours in the morning, always at exactly the same time, the Tedesci have their parade—their daily inspection. They are engaged until ten hours. Every one knows it is quite safe between eight and ten."

"He knew that well enough," put in Maria. "Would that one have stirred from the house if there had been the slightest risk to himself?"

Arnaldo nodded agreement.

"The reason he went out was because he knew it was quite safe at that time, and lying asleep upstairs on his bed, day after day, had begun to bore him."

Roberto disregarded these interruptions. "Realizing that some disguise was vital to my safety," he went on importantly, "I borrowed a pair of dark glasses that were upon the mantelpiece, and an old black coat——"

"He stole them when I was not looking," proclaimed Maria, "but when he got back, when he came creeping in, I was waiting for him at the door. I took them from him."

"I took the American across the square and then down

the street towards the fountain," continued Roberto. "It was my intention to take him to the house of my brother, Arnaldo, who would——"

"Brother-in-law," Arnaldo corrected.

Tommaso shook his clenched fist. "And then?" he demanded.

"Then, as we continued along the street, we came to the Casa Camerata. Francesca Camerata was standing in the doorway. The American made some remark which I did not comprehend, and gave a loud whistle." Roberto, his eyes watching the fermenting Tommaso, decided enough had been said. "That is all I know," he concluded rapidly.

"Liar!"

Don Leone intervened. "Tommaso! Control yourself!" he cried. "You are not charitable, you are thinking the worst of people. It is sinful——"

"What do I care for sins?" roared Tommaso. "You talk of sin at a time like this! Is this a time to be bringing in religion? I tell you I will have the truth." He shook his fist in Roberto's face. "Tell me the truth."

"I cannot. I do not know what it is. I am much upset," stuttered Roberto. "All I know is that the American began to talk to Francesca, and soon her mother, Signora Camerata, joined us. The American told them how he had descended from the air by means of a parachute, and many other things which I did not believe about his experiences in this terrible war. The signora and Francesca were much affected, they were very sympathetic. The American explained that he was seeking a lodging. He persuaded them to assist him."

Arnaldo nodded. "That seems probable. Remember he told us that before this war he was a salesman—a salesman of textiles. He would be accustomed to persuading women to overcome their reluctance."

Tommaso waved both his hands above his head. "An American living in the same house as Francesca! I will kill him!" he stormed.

"If you do not feel inclined to trust the American," urged Don Leone, "and perhaps it is not advisable to have an American in the same house———"

"Francesca is an attractive girl," agreed Arnaldo, "and it is well known what Americans do with attractive girls."

"—You could at least trust Francesca. She is a good girl, betrothed to you, Tommaso, and it is our duty to have faith, and to trust your future wife."

"Look here," said Kimber, who had been dodging about on the edge of the fray, "I don't exactly follow everything that's been said, but all this shouting is dangerous; you're simply asking for the Jerries to come here to find what it's all about." He took Tommaso's arm. "Simmer down, take it easy. All of you get so excited," he complained.

Roberto edged himself behind the priest. "It is now clear that I am in no way to blame," he said, resuming his own defence. "It would be satisfactory if Tommaso would realize that I have done nothing to distress him. I am the friend of every one, that is what should be understood, without doubt. The most important thing to realize is that if Tommaso feels concerned his anger should be against the American and every one else, but not against me. What I cannot understand is why Tommaso does not go boldly to the Casa Camerata, as I would do were I in his shoes, and confront the American with his misconduct."

"He has already been there," explained Don Leone. "He and the *capitano inglese* came down from the hills this evening, and then learnt where the American was lodged; as soon as he knew, Tommaso went immediately in great haste to the Casa Camerata."

"And what did I find?" demanded Tommaso. "That Francesca was out—gone for a walk—with the American!"

Arnaldo shook his head mournfully. "That was unsettling for Tommaso," he reasoned. "His concern can be understood. Every one knows what happens when a girl as attractive as Francesca goes for a walk with an American."

"That mother of hers," raged Tommaso; "I tried to get sense out of her, but she did not even know in which direction they had gone. But," he added with satisfaction, "I spoke to her! When I left she was in—what is the word, when a woman laughs in a shrieking tone and rat-tats her heels on the fender?"

"It was most embarrassing," said Kimber; "jolly awkward. I had to sprinkle water over the old girl."

"I will kill that American!" repeated Tommaso.

Kimber felt that the time had come to put the case logically, to present the facts. "You can't go killing people; there's a war on you know, and the war comes first," he reasoned. "You've got to realize our job is to blow up that bridge. It's a definite order, and that's what we're here for. After the bridge is destroyed we can go into this other matter, but our job comes first."

Tommaso waved him aside. "I am having no more to do with destroying our bridge. I refuse to lift a finger," he announced.

"Of that I approve," Arnaldo chipped in. "But I see

one insurmountable objection to your taking such an excellent course. Yesterday you told us you had received orders from the organization to assist and that if you did not obey two men would come from Turino and shoot you in the back of the head. I cannot see that any man could permit himself to be shot in the back of the head. It seems to me you have no option."

"What do I care for men from Turino!" shouted Tommaso. "It is I who will shoot them in the back of the head—yes, and in their stomachs, too."

There came a sharp knocking on the street door.

"God have mercy!" cried Roberto. "The Tedesci."

Arnaldo turned quickly to the window and peeped out. "It is worse," he remarked after a moment. "It is the American."

Tommaso sprang forward. "Let him in. Let me get at him"—then as Don Leone slipped in front of him and barred the way to the hall, he shouted, "Bring him in! I will kill him here!"

"Tommaso Ucelli, you will not," cried Maria, waddling over to the side of the priest. "Do you think I am going to have blood all over my clean floors? If you must kill him you will take him into the yard, where there is a drain and a floor of flags that can be washed."

Don Leone stood barring the way with Maria beside him.

"Tommaso," the priest said firmly, "you will listen to me and you will obey me. If you do not control yourself and do what I say you will bring disaster on us all. You will bring ruin not only on the *capitano inglese*, Arnaldo, and the good men in your organization and on their families, but you will bring misery to Francesca herself. The Tedesci have ways of making people talk, and once they get one person they will soon trace the others. It is for you to control yourself, and, whatever your feelings, do your duty, so that disaster does not fall upon us all."

He stood watching Tommaso for a few seconds, then continued, "We are now going to admit the American, and between us we will find some way to send him away from Fontana d'Amore. There will be an arrangement. It must be planned calmly, and we must subdue our personal feelings." Don Leone turned to Maria. "Go and open the front door," he said gently.

There was silence for a few moments, and then Bob Tuttle came into the room.

"Say, what's going on——"

"If you have any sense," interrupted Arnaldo, "you will say little; you will be most discreet. At the moment we are having great difficulty in preventing Tommaso here from cutting your throat."

"Now, listen here, lemme tell you . . ."

Kimber stepped forward. "I am in charge here," he said firmly. "You, Tommaso, and you, Sergeant Tuttle, are under my orders. Understand? I have been sent here to destroy that bridge and I'm going to do it. No one's personal feelings are going to stop the job being done. When that bridge is down you can cut each other's throats, or do just what you damn well please, but until then no one's going to spoil things."

When Kimber stopped speaking there was silence, then Arnaldo said meditatively, "Last night Tommaso went out over those rocks because he said if the body of the *capitano inglese* were found dead there would be searches, questioning, and our Resistance movement would be destroyed. To avoid this, Tommaso, who is a brave man, risked his life. If the body of the American sergeant were found, would not the same disasters come upon us?"

"Would you expect me to leave an American in the house of Francesca?" snapped Tommaso.

"Is that so? Lemme tell you . . ."

Tommaso and the American stood glaring at each other, the others—all except Roberto, whose intention it was to depart upstairs at the first sign of fighting—stood watching, ready to spring if a fight started.

"I wish," said Maria, "I had my rolling pin—the one I use when I make ravioli."

Don Leone hushed her with a gesture, and turning to Kimber, spoke to him in a low voice. "What we have got to do," he whispered, "is to find some way of returning the American sergeant to his people."

Kimber whispered that he did not see how this could be done. It was impossible to get an aircraft to come and pick up the American, and it would be more than difficult to pass him on foot through the German lines. "He will just have to stay until our crowd arrives here," he concluded.

Don Leone shook his head. "No," he said, "he cannot remain with the Cameratas; I could not accept the responsibility. Apart from the fact that it would be unwise, Tommaso would undoubtedly kill him, or they would do each other a serious injury. It is essential that we separate them. They must be put many miles apart."

A surge of exasperation swept Kimber's mind. He, who knew little of explosives, had been sent on this urgent and important mission. H.Q. had supported him with two sergeants, one of whom was out of action with a broken leg while the other was now apparently to be moved miles away. Then there was the stupidity of sending him signal flares instead of explosives—that was just inexcusable carelessness. And precious time was passing. Each night that the bridge remained standing meant so many more Jerries safely back across the river, ready to fight another day. Before he left H.Q., they had impressed upon him the importance of haste, had kept stressing the need for quick action. Kimber decided resentfully that he was not having a fair deal.

"I suppose," he said, looking hopelessly at the pugnacious Tommaso, "he won't simmer down in an hour or so?"

"As long as the American is anywhere near Fontana d'Amore," Arnaldo replied, "he will not compose himself. He will become increasingly cantankerous. It is only natural for him to feel that way. Francesca is his betrothed, and he could not be expected to allow her to be exposed to an American."

Don Leone agreed with a nod. "The American will have to be put in safe custody somewhere. What we have to decide is, where?"

"Say, now, jest you listen . . ."

Tommaso surged forward. "If he speaks," he shouted, "I will kill him! His voice enrages me, it will cause me to lose my temper."

The priest, Arnaldo, Maria, and Kimber closed in more firmly.

"I have it!" cried Don Leone suddenly. "I have the solution! The American can go to San Caprese."

"San Caprese," Arnaldo said thoughtfully. "Yes, certainly that would seem suitable. He could remain there in safety until the British arrive; of course that may not be for some months, but the air is good at San Caprese and would benefit him."

Tommaso, who had begun to look a little less savage added his opinion. "San Caprese is fifty kilometres from here. It would be difficult for him to sneak back; he would undoubtedly be shot on the way. Yes, if he is taken to San Caprese, and steps are taken to see he remains there, I will accept the arrangement."

Only Roberto seemed doubtful. "It is not a place in which I should like to find myself," he commented. "For me, it would not be agreeable."

But Kimber, who was ready to grasp at any straw that seemed to offer a solution, ignored the unfavourable opinion. He looked at Tommaso.

"If Sergeant Tuttle goes to this place—what's it's name?—will you settle down and get on peacefully with blowing up that bridge?"

Tommaso hesitated. "I do not wish to assist in destroying . . ." he began. "But no matter. If this snake goes to San Caprese at once, starts now, Arnaldo can take him; then I will stifle my inclinations, I will not cut his throat, I will assist you."

"See here, you guys——"

"Sergeant Tuttle," said Kimber, "you are under my orders. You will go to . . . er . . . San Caprese and remain there until either we send for you or our troops reach there. That is an order."

Don Leone moved towards his desk. "I will write a note," he said, "explaining what is required. There will be no difficulty, the Abbot is a hospitable soul; although somewhat formidable, he will, I know, give you"—he bowed slightly to Sergeant Tuttle—"accommodation for as long as may be required."

"Say, are you all crazy? I'm not a sap——"

"You are coming with me," said Arnaldo. "As soon as

we have Don Leone's note we start walking; it will be a long walk. If we are fortunate we should get there by tomorrow night."

"I feel it is somewhat unkind," Roberto remarked, "to send our American cousin to San Caprese. As I said, I should not find a stay there—even of one day—agreeable."

"It would be the best thing for you," Maria put in. "You should have been sent there long ago."

Kimber felt a certain curiosity. "Just what is this place?" he asked.

It was Tommaso who replied, and there was a grim satisfaction in his voice.

"San Caprese is a monastery right up in the mountains," he said. "It is more than ten kilometres from the nearest village. It is of an order of monks most austere."

"Holy smoke!" exclaimed Sergeant Tuttle, leaping as if a pin had pricked him, "say, listen here, lemme tell you . . ."

7

The Explosion

THERE ARE SOME MEN WHO, WHEN ENGAGED IN AN important enterprise, pause periodically and review what has so far happened and the progress that has been made. It was to this class of methodical persons that Roy Kimber belonged. As he and Tommaso sat, in silence among the bracken, waiting for Giovanni to bring the explosives which H.Q. in their radio message had promised they would send that night, Kimber was busy compiling a mental balance sheet of the whole situation.

The time that had already been lost was the most unfortunate factor. When Kimber had been called to H.Q. and the enterprise explained to him it had been made very clear that what was needed was a quick survey followed by prompt action. The staff officer had been emphatic. "The longer that bridge is left standing, the more time the Jerries have to get stuff away—stuff they'll use against us farther back. Every hour matters. Every hour that bridge is usable strengthens the Jerries. Every hour is important." And the colonel who had been present at the interview had concurred. He had said, "Oh, yes, dashed important."

When Kimber had started to ask questions as to the details of the job he had to do the staff officer had cut him short. "If you're in any doubt when you get there we can always send you instructions by radio. Can't hold things up for that now. Besides, we don't quite know what *is* the situation on the spot. The main thing is to get you there quick."

The Italian Resistance had sent their radio call on Monday, and it was now Thursday. That interview at H.Q. had been four days ago. Yet Kimber did not feel it was he who was to blame for the delay. A few hours after he had been dropped he had made a complete recce of the bridge and its surroundings; that night he had made his first attempt to destroy the bridge. The attempt had failed, not through any fault of his, but because H.Q. had sent him signal flares instead of explosives. True, the Italian fellow forgetting to charge the battery had also hampered things, and that might be considered partly Kimber's fault, but even if the battery had worked . . . Of course, if he or either of the sergeants sent to support him had been experts in sabotage, or even had some superficial knowledge of the subject, they would have recognized the signal flares for what they were, and some time might have been saved, and certainly some danger to personnel avoided. But you could not blame Kimber for that. He had told the staff officer that he had received no training in demolition and had little experience with explosives. The staff officer had just replied, "H'm, pity! but you'll manage O.K., I'm sure. It's quite simple, really— not difficult, you know." And the colonel had added, "Just a matter of common sense."

At the end of the interview Kimber had ventured to ask—at the risk of them thinking he wished to shirk the job—why "P" Staff had selected him. The colonel had replied that they needed some one who was good at Italian. It was a rush job, and they had just told "P" staff to pick a parachute bloke from the transit camp who could speak Italian. Kimber had not liked to admit that his ability to speak Italian might have its weaknesses, but he did mention again that his knowledge of explosives was elementary.

Reviewing his selection impartially, Kimber decided it was possible that "P" Staff could have made a better choice.

The selection of those two sergeants, thought Kimber, had also not been too clever. He had asked if he could meet the sergeants, who were to join him, and satisfy himself that they were suitable. But the staff officer had explained the sergeants had not yet arrived. "The whole thing has been dumped on us so quickly, and we've got to get something started immediately, that we just haven't time for careful selection and proper briefing—it's a rush job; you'll have to go there and sort things out when you know what's needed." It might be unfair to blame "P" Staff, but the position now was that out of the two men H.Q. had sent to support him, one was in hospital—or rather, in a cowshed, which was temporarily being used as a hospital—and the other was entering a monastery.

However, no good going into that; he was here in Fontana d'Amore, and his job was to get that bridge blown up without any more delay. H.Q. had radioed that they were dropping the correct type of explosive tonight, and at any time Giovanni should arrive with them. Kimber peered at his wrist-watch—the time was nearly one o'clock. Giovanni was late. No good worrying; when he did come they would all set off for the bridge and, with Tommaso and Giovanni to help him, Kimber would finish the job.

All the same, thought Kimber, he did hope H.Q. would have the sense to send some kind of instructions with the explosives, as to how they should be treated. A book of words would be useful.

Tommaso started to speak. "I was perhaps somewhat annoyed about that American," he murmured, "but now I no longer feel concern. By to-morrow night Arnaldo, if he walks briskly, will have got him to San Caprese, and once there he will be out of the way."

"You don't think the American will come back?"

"If he does, then I will cut his throat," Tommaso replied placidly. "But there is little chance of his returning. I gave Arnaldo instructions as to what he should tell the monks. I told him to say they were to invite the American to have a bath. It is well known that Americans are fond of baths, and after such a long walk it is probable he would accept such an offer. I requested that when he was in the bath one of the monks must collect the American's trousers and put them in safe custody. It is most unlikely that even an American would undertake a walk of more than fifty kilometres, back to Fontana d'Amore, if he lacked trousers."

"But, I say," exclaimed Kimber, somewhat startled, "it may be a month or more before our people get as far north as this; the monks can't keep him without trousers for a month!"

"I do not see why there should be any difficulty about doing so. Those monks are very austere; they live in great simplicity and get much enjoyment from penances. They are great advocates of penances, and I am sure they would regard it as a penance for the American to be without trousers. They would explain to him it was reparation for his sins."

Kimber and Tommaso lapsed into silence again, and for more than five minutes neither spoke. Then the faint sound of some one walking cautiously up the path came to them.

"Giovanni," whispered Tommaso, "but hush until we are sure."

They heard the walker stop for a few moments, then begin to scramble up the bank towards them, through the bracken.

"Where," Kimber began, as Giovanni reached them and he saw that the man was empty handed, "where are the explosives?"

"I have not got them with me, *capitano*. I did not bring them because—do not be disappointed, *capitano*—they have not arrived."

"Not arrived? D'you mean you couldn't find the parachute?"

"Had there been a parachute we should have found it; we are well experienced in such work and realize the danger of leaving an unfound parachute about for the Tedesci to discover. But be consoled—I have with me a message that came on the radio at twenty-two hundred hours, as was promised. It has been decoded and written clearly. It is here."

He held out a sheet of paper.

Kimber peered, trying to read the words on the paper. "I can't see a thing," he muttered.

"Bend low on to the ground," said Tommaso. "I will put my coat over your head. Here is my torch. Do not switch it on until I have you covered."

Enveloped in the coat, Kimber switched on the torch and—holding the paper in his other hand—read the message.

   Most secret memorize only destroy immediately stop can not repeat not deliver canisters to-night stop essential destruction be completed immediately stop improvise with materials obtained locally stop you will complete mission at once stop further delay most serious and will not be tolerated stop message ends.

Kimber wriggled from the covering coat. "Here," he said bitterly, "just read this."

Tommaso burrowed under the coat. There was a glimmer of the torch for a little time, and then Tommaso reappeared.

"What the hell do they mean?" demanded Kimber. " 'Improvise with materials obtained locally.' Do they expect me to borrow a pickaxe, and start digging the damned bridge to pieces? 'Complete mission at once.' I never heard such rot! As if I wasn't doing all . . . Oh, blast the lot of 'em!"

Tommaso remained silent.

"How can I get on with the job if they don't send me explosives?" fumed Kimber. "Whose fault is it? Improvise! Do they expect me to walk into some shop and say 'give me three hundred-weights of explosive—the best quality, please?' Oh, to hell with the lot of them!"

"You are becoming displeased, *capitano*, but you should not do so. You should remain benevolent."

"Look here, did they or did they not send the wrong things? Didn't they mess up the whole show? And now they talk about delay and 'will not be tolerated.' I tell you, I'm bloody well fed up!"

"Remain calm, *capitano*. When annoyances happen it is best to laugh indulgently."

"You're a nice one to talk!"

Tommaso took the words as a compliment. "I appreciate that you think so," he said, bowing.

What was he to do? Kimber asked himself. What was

the next move? All this stuff about improvising was just
damned silly. How could he wreck the bridge without explosives, and how could he possibly obtain explosives
out here in the countryside? "I suppose," he said bitterly,
"they think I might go to the Jerries and ask them to lend
me a ton or two."

The only course, decided Kimber at last, was to send
a message through on that radio, tell the blighters plainly
that unless they sent him explosives he could not do a
thing; tell 'em to get busy and put a jerk in it. But even
if they did act quickly, think how much time had been
lost. It was now nearly two o'clock in the morning, and
by the time he had drafted a message and the 'Eye-ties'
had put it into code and sent it off it would be daylight.
So no explosives could be expected before to-morrow
night, and that was Friday night—five nights since the
'Eye-ties' had first warned H.Q. It was not his fault if
precious time had been wasted. They couldn't blame him
—although judging by the last message, that was exactly
what they seemed to be doing.

Kimber explained briefly what were his plans.

Tommaso considered the matter. "The next time at
which we can transmit is . . . let me see . . ."—he counted
on his fingers—"twelve hundred hours; that is in ten
hours time, so you will not be forced to hurry in com-
posing the message."

Kimber grunted.

"It will be daylight soon, *capitano*," continued Tommaso, "and so what I propose is that all three of us now
set off walking to the Hermitage. I do not like using the
same resting-place two days in succession, but the Hermitage is convenient, and perhaps it will be safe to risk
it. When we are settled for the day you can compose

your letter, and then Giovanni will take it to be coded and despatched at twelve hundred hours. Now, come, let us start walking."

As they trudged upward into the hills, Kimber's mind was busy trying to frame a message that, while terse, would explain the position and yet express something of his feelings. 'Disgusted at . . .' No, that would not do. 'What the hell . . .' Yes—expressive, but unwise. 'Of all the blasted . . .' Not likely to make friends and influence people. A difficult message to compose, he decided.

So Kimber, Tommaso, and Giovanni trudged on towards the Hermitage.

It was nearly midday when Kimber stirred on his bed of straw in the corner of the Hermitage and saw Tommaso sitting upright at the door munching a slice of bread covered with slices of bacon.

"I haven't overslept?"

"You have half an hour yet. Be assured I should have disturbed you at the proper time."

The warm sunlight spread from the open door, brightening the inside of the little room. Through the doorway Kimber could see the green of the pine-trees and above the tips of these the cloudless blue sky. A lark spiralled high into the air, and, as it rose, its song sounded like a soothing lullaby.

"Not a bad place, this," said Kimber, who had wakened feeling more tranquil, "sort of peaceful. A lot worse places than this."

Tommaso ignored the comment. To him such remarks were unnecessary. That there were worse places was, of course, indisputable, but he could think of many more pleasant places where he would like to be. To be spending his time hidden in a Hermitage that at night—and who could be certain not also in the daytime?—was haunted by a ghost, was not his idea of good living. There was also the risk that the Tedesci had, in one way or another, obtained information and might appear at any moment—a possibility that Tommaso considered would be disturbing.

"*Capitano*," Tommaso said at last, "while you have been sleeping, and while I have been on watch, I have been thinking of that message you had dispatched to your superiors. I have been wondering if it was a wise one to send? I do not fully comprehend what will be the feelings of British officers when they receive it, but in our army such a message would be considered discourteous, and our superior officers would be much affronted."

Kimber, who had himself begun to have faint doubts about the matter, and was inclined to think the message might perhaps have been worded more tactfully, grunted, "Well, they asked for it. Talking about improvising, and all that."

Tommaso remained silent for a few moments, then said, "*Capitano*, I would be distressed if you were to find yourself in any trouble. I would be concerned deeply if your superior officers became enraged. Tell me, is it likely they will feel you have not been eager in the matter of destroying our bridge? In the Italian army, if anyone is suspected of not being wholehearted he is immediately sent away to fight the Russians. It would distress me if you, *capitano*, were sent by your authorities to Russia, where it is very beastly, and where there is much cruelty."

"Oh, there won't be any chance of my being posted to Russia—at least, I don't think so. Of course 'P' Staff are capable of messing anything up, but I don't believe even they would think of Russia. Anyway the Russians are sort of Allies of ours."

"But your superior officers are not pleased? They are in a fury with you?" persisted Tommaso.

"Well," said Kimber slowly, "well, from their last message it does rather look as if they thought I wasn't pulling my weight. But—what the hell—it was they who sent the wrong stuff. Improvise! How could I get explosives here?"

A certain embarrassment seemed to come over Tommaso. He seemed as if he were going to say something, then he hesitated. It was nearly a minute before he said tentatively, "Perhaps I have not been fully frank with you, *capitano*, but I would ask you to remember what a disaster the destruction of our bridge would be to all people; knowing the misery it would bring has perhaps influenced me unduly."

"The Jerries would have blown it up when they left," replied Kimber. "One of us was going to do it anyway."

"That is true, your failure has only postponed the evil," Tommaso went on quietly. "It was because I kept hoping that in some way something would happen to stop both of you from bringing this calamity upon us that I was not fully frank." He drew himself up. He had made his decision. "Yes, I will tell you. When your superior officers ordered that you were to do what they named 'improvise' they intended that you should use the facilities that were already here."

"What? You haven't any explosives here?"

Tommaso sighed. "Ah, yes, *capitano*—at least, our organization itself does not possess any, but around here there are—as you will have seen—many stone quarries. In these quarries work many men who are accustomed

to using powerful explosives. To such men the destruction of the bridge would have presented no difficulty.
Some of these men are of the Resistance."

"Oh, gosh!"

"It would be a simple matter for one of these men—
Giuseppe Bocci, for instance—to break into the shed in
which the explosives live. He would know exactly what
materials were required, and he is highly skilled at blowing things up. He has been destroying things ever since he
was a child. I remember one day at school Giuseppe, he
take a——"

"You mean this Giuseppe has explosives and knows
how to use them?"

"He does not actually possess explosives at the
moment, but he works in a quarry and knows well the
building in which the explosives are kept. Of course the
building is kept locked most strictly, but Giuseppe has
often entered buildings which were locked against him.
Before the war it was a habit of his to do so, and five
times the Carabinieri succeeded in proving this. On each
occasion he was sent to prison at Sulmona, but there
were many, many times when the Carabinieri could
prove nothing. Giuseppe would have no difficulty in getting whatever explosives were desired, and when he has
them he is an expert in their use."

Kimber did not speak for a few moments. Then, "Well,
I'm damned," he said at last.

"I tell you this, *capitano*, only because I feel your
superior officers are aware of this facility we have at our
disposal and that they could be enraged with you because you did not use it," concluded Tommaso. "In my
own case, if I failed the superior officers in our organization two men would come from Turino. I have a liking

for you, *capitano*, and I would not wish two men to come from London and shoot you in the back of the head."

Kimber made up his mind quickly, explained his plan, and gave his orders. Tommaso was to go at once to find Giuseppe, instruct him to obtain the explosives soon after dark, and bring them to the meeting-place on the path near the bridge at one hundred hours.

"To-night we'll finish the job," he pronounced. "It's almost too late, but we'll get it done to-night, certain."

Five minutes later Tommaso had departed on his mission, and Kimber took his place at the doorway watching and listening.

It was maddening, thought Kimber, that Tommaso had waited until now to disclose information about the quarries and the men who not only could obtain explosives but who understood how to use them. Four—no—five valuable days had been lost, and all this time the Jerries had been withdrawing men and material across the bridge. Curse Tommaso! Of course, to be fair, he, Kimber, ought to have realized the possibilities of those quarries. He had been sent to destroy the bridge and was in command; it was his show; he was here to plan things and say what was to be done. You could not really blame Tommaso, he was an 'Eye-tie', and all these 'Eye-ties' were dead against blowing up the bridge. After all, it did mean the end of their town and the finish of their land in the valley. It was going to be a disaster for them. But what were H.Q. going to think—and say— about Kimber? You could understand now why their message had been a bit shirty. They were feeling that he had done a poor show. Still, H.Q. were a lot to blame. Why had they picked a chap who knew almost nothing about this sabotage stuff? One of those highly trained

Commando fellows, who understood all about detonators, fuses, and things like that, was the type they should have sent. It was one muddle after another—always muddling through.

These Italians, Kimber decided, were a strange race. Tommaso, for example, keeping back the vital information about the quarries and then suddenly telling the whole story just because he thought Kimber might get into trouble. Here was a man who, while detesting the idea of blowing up the bridge and admitting that he was very frightened, had insisted that he should be the one to carry those canisters and cables across the bare rocks to within yards of German machine-guns.

People thought of Italians as romantic, and, in a way, they were, but almost every Italian was fundamentally a realist—he saw the actual facts of a situation logically and clearly. Some people thought Italians lacked courage, and when they were compelled to fight for a cause which their reason told them was unsound, no doubt they did try to save their own skins. But the average Italian, fighting for what his reason tells him is sound, hating danger, and envisaging, with vivid imagination, the risks, is nevertheless brave. He goes ahead with the courage of a man afraid, yet who will not turn back.

Kimber remembered some Italian prisoners he had talked to in North Africa. "I am not in agreement with Fascism," one had said. "I do not approve of this war, and anyway I think we are on the wrong side. I am therefore not going to give my life for a Government I do not like and a war I do not support, so at the first opportunity I have become a prisoner; that is the sensible way to behave."

The average Briton, Kimber thought, did not reason in

that way. He went on fighting because of a sense of loyalty to those around him. He called it "not letting the side down." Lacking a vivid imagination, he did not visualize in the clearest detail, as the Italian did, the searing pain that would come when his flesh was torn apart. He just tried to convince himself that he might be one of the lucky ones that would come through unscathed.

All through the long afternoon Kimber waited in the Hermitage, sometimes sitting at the doorway, sometimes taking a few steps about the room. The glorious view of the mountains and the perfect picture of the valley failed to soothe him, and even the gentle sunlight seemed to add to his frustration. He wished that it would rain hard.

It was nearly six o'clock when there came the sound of a rustle in the bracken and Tommaso returned.

"Well?" demanded Kimber.

"I have arranged it. I have seen Giuseppe. At first he did not desire to become embroiled, but I mentioned to him one or two matters about himself which he would not wish to have known; I explained that he had no option. In the end he agreed to assist us."

"He is getting the right explosives?"

"Assuredly. About twenty-three hundred hours he will enter the building where the explosives live; then he will select what is most desirable and bring these to our meeting-place. He will be there at one hundred hours."

"Good."

"At first he was most reluctant. He has great fear of the Tedesci and even more of the Carabinieri, who, he says, do not regard him with fairness. He asked to be excused when he had brought the materials to us. I had to make it plain that he could not behave in this way."

"He will turn up all right?"

"Senza dubbio. I was courteous, but he understood what I would do to him if he failed."

Tommaso sat down on the bed.

"You're tired out," said Kimber. "Why don't you have a sleep?"

"Yes, I am very tired," Tommaso agreed. "But I dare not sleep. We must be away from here soon. In another hour it will be dark, and to remain here then would be highly dangerous and most unwise." He stretched himself in the straw. "Yes, in another hour we must leave, certainly. Once it is dark, the ghost could appear. I have no wish to meet the ghost. It is well known that these apparitions bring ill luck; besides, I have a distaste for such persons."

Kimber sat at the door thinking. It did look as if to-night would see the end of the business. An experienced quarryman with the proper explosives could hardly fail. By to-morrow morning the bridge would be destroyed. It was a pity this long delay had occurred. The Jerries must have got a lot of stuff away in the last five days. H.Q. were going to be pretty worked up about that. Still, the job was now nearly finished.

Kimber watched the darkening sky, the deep orange of the sunset.

"I do not feel it would be safe for us to stay here longer," said Tommaso, breaking the silence and starting to rise from the bed. "It is now getting dark. Darkness comes suddenly, and it is not quite certain that the ghost confines himself entirely to this one building. It is said that he has also been met upon the path near by. I think we should now leave."

As the evening turned to night, they set off through the bracken, then down the path leading to the valley.

Half an hour's walking brought them to a little cluster of buildings—a small farmstead. Tommaso crouched down among the lines of vines, and for perhaps ten minutes he and Kimber watched in silence. At last he stood up and began to walk cautiously towards the door of the farmhouse. "This is Giovanni's home," he told Kimber. "We will be able to have a meal and rest here, until it is time for us to go to meet Giuseppe near the bridge." Reaching the door, Tommaso did not knock, but opened it a few inches, and stood for a moment looking into the farm kitchen.

A welcome smell of cooking *pasta* came to them. A stout woman in a black dress was standing by the stove. "Buona sera," she said, with a smile. "We were expecting you."

"Buona sera," replied Tommaso, and stepping into the room, motioned Kimber to follow him. "This is the *capitano inglese*—this is Signora Giovanni."

The woman wiped her hand on a cloth and turned to shake hands with Kimber. "You are very welcome," she told him, smiling. "I am most fond of the British and also the Highlanders and the Welsh. For five years before I was married I worked in the house of a British family who resided at Firenze. They were very rich, but quite civilized when you got to know them. Not so some of their friends who came to stay. Some of these were from London; they were not civilized. Do you come from London, *capitano*?"

Kimber murmured something about his home being in Wiltshire.

Signora Giovanni went on talking as she bustled about preparing the meal. "It will be ready soon, so do not distress yourself, *capitano*. A little while, and you will be sitting down in peace. Ah, yes, peace; peace is what we want, is it not? I have no patience with this silly war——"

"Where is Giovanni?" Tommaso interrupted.

"He is in the haystack."

To Kimber the inside of a haystack seemed a strange place for a man to spend his time.

The signora saw Kimber's surprise and laughed. "He is playing with his radio," she explained. "When the radio visits us we keep it in the haystack, and he is out there playing with it now."

"I told you we move the radio from place to place," explained Tommaso grumpily. "Here the haystack is a wise situation."

"It must be worrying for you, signora—all this under-cover stuff, I mean. You must be anxious?"

The woman lifted a fork bearing strands of *pasta* up and down above the steaming pan. "A few more minutes, *capitano*." She glanced at the table and murmured to herself, "Bread, wine, butter, cheese"; then she replied to Kimber's question. "Anxious? Ah, yes, at times I am. Giovanni is not strong, and being out in the nights in all weathers is not beneficial to him. But he enjoys it. It keeps him occupied. And so I say it is better for him to play at that——"

"You talk as if it were a game," said Tommaso re-provingly. "I do not wish to speak as Roberto would do, but we of the Resistance take considerable risks; we are often in great danger."

The signora continued to flutter around the stove. "Of course you do," she said, as if soothing a child. Then, smiling at Kimber, she explained, "Men never grow up, they remain as little boys. To have this Resistance, as they call it, pleases them. They greatly enjoy playing with such things."

Kimber thought of Tommaso crawling over the rocks by the river, and of his own feelings when he was doing that parachute jump. He felt that Signora Giovanni had not quite the right idea, but before he could put his thoughts into words the door opened and Giovanni came in.

"All is well," he announced.

His wife cut him short. "The *pasta* is nearly ready. Wash your hands and brush yourself down. You cannot sit at the table with a Britisher in that state. And remember your manners. You have had your fun, now behave properly."

"Did you send that message of mine?" whispered Kimber.

"It went at twelve hundred hours, nine hours ago," Giovanni replied. He caught his wife's glance, stepped quickly towards the sink, and started to wash his hands. "Two replies came back at nineteen hundred hours."

"Two?"

"Yes, two. I decoded them, I have them here," said Giovanni, drying himself on the towel. He felt in his pockets, and then produced two sheets of paper. Kimber snatched them and, spreading the messages on one corner of the table, started to read. Tommaso, leaning over his shoulder, read the messages at the same time. The first sheet said:

Most secret memorize only destroy immediately stop regret failure to deliver stop those responsible reprimanded stop correct materials being dropped Sunday night stop place and time will be notified stop your actions approved conduct considered highly satisfactory in difficult circumstances stop have full confidence in you message ends.

"I am relieved," said Tommaso. "It is clear your superior officers are not enraged. Had I known I would not have mentioned Giuseppe or the quarries."

"I must keep that message, it might come in useful," murmured Kimber.

Tommaso looked doubtful. "But, *capitano*," he said, "it instructs 'destroy immediately.' "

"Oh, no one takes any notice of that stuff," said Kimber.

They both started to read the second message.

Most secret memorize only destroy immediately stop mission must repeat must be completed immediately stop delay highly unsatisfactory stop you will take immediate action stop your last message insubordinate stop your replacement and recall under consideration stop message ends.

There was a pause, and then Tommaso said, "I am glad that I mentioned Giuseppe and the quarries."

"Both messages came together," Giovanni volunteered, "one after another."

Kimber nodded. "I bet two different sections sent them. The thing that matters is who sent which."

Tommaso looked puzzled. "I do not fully comprehend you. But it seems to me your superior officers are like ours—they do not let their right ear hear what has been audible to their left."

"Put those papers away!" Signora Giovanni broke in sharply. "You can look at them afterwards. Do you realize the food is waiting on the table? After all the trouble I have taken, would you let it go cold?"

The three men sat down hurriedly and drew their plates towards them, with a sense of guilt.

"Now, you've not to leave any," the signora admonished them. "It is good food—as good as can be obtained during this wretched war—and will do you good. Eat it up while it is hot."

In silence the men started forking the *pasta* from their plates.

Although he was worried about those two messages, and also felt it necessary to behave carefully so that no action of his should bring a reproof from the signora— who obviously regarded the three men and spoke to them as if they were boys of ten—Kimber thoroughly enjoyed that meal. The *pasta* had that rich flavour that *pasta* has only in Italy, the shredded cheese a sharp tang that made the dish wholly appetizing. The slices of bread with which they mopped up the tomato sauce on their plates were fresh and crisp. The fruit and the wine, both products of the farm, tasted magnificent. It was a jolly meal, the signora smiling and tolerant, looking after them like a good mother, Giovanni and Tommaso, apparently their anxieties forgotten, chuckling and reminiscing about past adventures.

Cheered by the happy surroundings and the good wine, Kimber began to feel jovial as the meal ended, his cares began to slip away. What did it matter about H.Q? To hell with them all! He drained another glass of wine and began to peel an orange. It was grand in here, he thought; warm, comfortable, good food, cheerful companions. Really, these Italians, when you got to know them, were a jolly good crowd. Kind, and all that. He liked them. "Vostra salute," he said, as Giovanni filled his glass again. It was a rotten thing, blowing up that bridge.

That bridge was a great work of art, a beautiful thing. That fellow—what's his name—was quite right; it was like destroying a great painting, like going into the National Gallery and chucking acid at a priceless masterpiece. H.Q. had no right to go about blowing up beautiful paintings.

As he pressed the orange, spots of juice shot up on to Kimber's cheek. He laughed heartily and took another drink of wine. Bad show, he decided. Bringing ruin on a whole countryside, washing away all that soil, wrecking the lives of decent people like these. A damned shame, smashing up people's homes and livelihoods.

Giovanni pushed his chair back and stood up. "I will now sing," he announced. "I will sing for our friend, the *capitano inglese*, an old Tuscan love-song——"

"You will do no such thing!" said the signora. "Sit down at once!"

Giovanni sat down.

"Such manners! What will the *capitano* think!"

"I think," said the *capitano*, bowing, "Giovanni's a damned good sort, also you, Tommaso, and you, of course, signora—all good sorts."

Kimber began to hum a catchy little tune he had heard on his way up through Italy. After tackling the first line in Italian, he switched over to a free translation. "Non dimenticare mie parole . . . My little darling sweetheart, you are sweeter than the sun . . ."

"Good, good," cried Giovanni, "the *capitano* is musical. As I told you, he would like to hear an old song of Tuscany."

"He would do nothing of the kind! You will take no more wine; it is, as it always does, affecting you."

"I do not think," Tommaso supported the signore, "it

would be either wise or agreeable if you, Giovanni, were to start singing."

A silence came on the party, and Kimber resumed his thoughts.

That fellow—what was his name? Roberto, yes, that was it—Roberto. Good old Roberto was quite right, it was sacrilege, vandalism. Just not done. This blowing up works of art, things that could never be replaced, was a damned shame.

"Vostra salute," said Kimber, again emptying his glass.

And those blasted Jerries too—they were going to blow up the picture; just the sort of beastly, brutal, barbarous thing Jerries would do. But were they? For two pins, Kimber thought, he would go down there and knock the stuffing out of them, knock the lot of them for six; hold the bloody bridge until the British came. That was the way to deal with the situation—hold the bridge intact so that the British could use it when they advanced. Why the hell hadn't H.Q. thought of that? Proper thing to do. No question about it.

"Vostra salute," said Kimber, rising to his feet. "I will now make a speech, a *discorso*." He laughed heartily. "Yes, a *discorso*, in Italian. Senza dubbio, domani, buona sera, arrivederci." Convulsed with laughter he had to pause.

"Good, good," shouted Giovanni, "and I will sing an old Tuscan love-song. After which I will perform my dance upon the table."

Before the signora could correct her husband, Kimber continued with his speech. "My dear friends, my very dear friends, for we are friends—say what you like, we are friends. I have always said the 'Eye-ties' were our friends, not a fighting race—run away as soon as the shooting starts—but still our friends . . ."

Signora Giovanni had been watching Kimber for some time, now she was sure. She spoke sharply. "The *capitano inglese* is not to have any more wine. Take his glass away."

Before anyone could move, Kimber lifted his glass and drained it, then grinned reassuringly at the signora. "All O.K.," he said, smiling pleasantly, "all under control. Vostra salute!" Then, looking down, he saw Tommaso sitting beside him. "What! you still here?" he said, in surprise. "I thought you'd gone ages ago. Mustn't hang about here, you know. Ghost may come. Ghost may turn up at any minute."

"There is no ghost in residence here," replied Tommaso reprovingly.

"Never know, old boy—popping in an' out all over the place, these ghosts. My old grandmother—she was a Macdonald—often saw ghosts. They were great pals of hers and warned her about her friends, when the friends were going to die, and things like that. . . ."

There was a hurried conference between the signora and Tommaso.

Hearing their remarks, Giovanni tried to be helpful. "It might soothe his mind," he suggested, "if I were encouraged to sing an old Tuscan love-song, and afterwards to dance upon——"

"Will you be quiet!" snapped the signora.

"In two hours," said Tommaso solemnly, "we have to meet Giuseppe."

Kimber put his hand on Tommaso's shoulder and addressed him earnestly. " 'Hail to thee, blithe Spirit,

Bird thou never wert . . .' and don't you go on worrying about ghosts."

Signora Giovanni decided that action, not words, was what was necessary. She issued her orders. "He must lie down," she commanded. "A sleep is what he needs, poor soul. I will get him some strong coffee." Then, turning on her husband, she exploded, "It is your fault for rushing him about the hills day after day with no proper food, never giving him a moment's rest. Wait until I tell Father Leone of your behaviour."

"It is unjust to blame me," protested Giovanni. "If I had been permitted to soothe him with a song . . ."

"Friends," chuckled Kimber, "all my friends."

"You will lie down," the signora ordered. "Do you hear me?"

"Tell you what I've decid—decid— Made up my mind. Not going to blow up that bridge. Not doing it. Damned shame."

"Put him in that chair before the fire," said the signora. "Put his feet up."

With some difficulty Tommaso persuaded Kimber to be helped to the chair beside the wood fire.

The signora hurried off to make coffee.

"Not going to blow up works of art. Not doing it. Made up my mind. All over."

Tommaso looked at Kimber sternly. "At one hundred hours we have to meet Giuseppe," he reminded him. "You have been sent here with orders to destroy our bridge. If you do not carry out your orders two men from London will arrive and shoot you in the back of the head. I cannot accept that happening."

"Not blowing up bridge."

"You will do your duty. You will carry out your

orders. I will not have men from London coming here to shoot you."

"Not blowing up——"

"Then I will do it myself," said Tommaso firmly. "I cannot let a man be shot because he sees things foolishly owing to a little too much wine. The bridge will be blown up."

The signora at the stove turned her head. "You are just a lot of children," she commented. "It is as my mother always said, men never grow up. I have said it myself a thousand times. They remain boys and play at silly games."

"In two hours' time we have to meet Giuseppe," said Tommaso. "Make that coffee strong while I put a wet cloth over his face."

It was past midnight when Tommaso and Kimber reached the path near the bridge, where they were to meet Giuseppe. Kimber had a racking headache and his legs still felt weak and wobbly, but the rest by the fire, the strong coffee, and, most of all, the stern disapproval of the signora had done much to bring him back to his normal self. Also the walk in the fresh night air, from the farmstead to the meeting-place, had benefited him considerably.

Kimber sat in silence, and although thought was not easy, he began to survey the situation. H.Q. had said they would drop the correct explosives on Sunday night. That could be too late. If Tommaso's information was correct the Jerries had already withdrawn a lot of men and materials. By Sunday morning—Tommaso was sure—they would have little further use for the bridge and might destroy it at any time. Even if the Jerries did not act before Sunday night, and if H.Q. did send the right stuff and Kimber did the job successfully, it would be a case of closing the door after the horse had gone. Time was running out. The only chance left was that this Giuseppe fellow would bring the right explosives to-night and explain how to set them off. Everything now depended on Giuseppe. To-night was the last chance.

Gosh, he had a headache! Every time he moved his head it was like————

"You are quite sure the Jerries are nearly ready to clear out?"

Tommaso nodded. "For the last three nights," he said, "we have had watchers counting the number of trucks. You have seen the figures yourself. Hardly any vehicles have come south, but many, many have gone north. Besides, it is clear from other information that the Tedesci are almost finished here."

"It almost seems purposeless going on."

"We have to go on. Even if we do not destroy the bridge the Tedesci will. We cannot stop them. If we could stop them . . . Ah, that would be a great blessing. Much thought has been given to ways of stopping them, but there is no way."

Kimber pressed his hands to his forehead.

"As we cannot stop the Tedesci," Tommaso continued, "it is you, *capitano*, who are my concern. That message from your superior officers was discourteous; it is clear that they are enraged with you. The only way to appease them will be for you to act before the Tedesci. To-night could be our last opportunity————" He suddenly stopped speaking, as a loud crash split the silence, the echoes booming among the mountains.

"Mother of Mercy, what is that!"

"They've done it," said Kimber. "The Jerries have——"

"No, it came from the hills, not from the bridge. Look, you can see the bridge is intact."

Kimber turned his head quickly and wished that he had not done so. "A bomb," he suggested. "Some plane's dropped a bomb."

"We must get out of here rapidly," said Tommaso, jumping to his feet. "The Tedesci will start searching."

Kimber stood up slowly.

"*Capitano*, come swiftly. We shall have the Tedesci here."

Tommaso started to hurry back along the path. Kimber followed him. For perhaps ten minutes they trotted in silence; then Tommaso spoke again.

"I saw a flash. It was in the direction of Giovanni's farm."

Kimber did not reply. The jolting over the uneven ground had stirred up the agonizing pain in his head. This walking, he decided, was just hell.

The sound of some one coming quickly down the path towards them caused Tommaso to pause and draw Kimber into the shadow of the bushes. The steps became louder, and a figure showed in the darkness.

"Giovanni!"

Giovanni stopped, breathless.

"Thank Our Lady I have found you!" he panted. "I have prayed to her——"

"What has happened?"

"It is Giuseppe. He has blown himself up."

"Killed?"

"Not completely. But he was much distressed. Now he is running very fast up into the hills. I had to come to find you, to tell you you must get right away with speed. The Tedesci will be everywhere."

"Of that I am fully aware," Tommaso replied. "Quick —what happened?"

"Giuseppe, he gets the materials, and I meet him as was arranged to guide him to you. I was walking ahead of him. What occurred I do not know, but there was, without warning, a great flash and a terrible roar. I was caused much vexation. I fell flat upon the ground. When I recovered I found Giuseppe jumping about and giving shrill exclamations, for the explosion had set fire to his trousers. I endeavoured to calm him, but he would not be reasonable; he was excited, and made it clear he would assist us no further. He is now running with great speed away into the hills."

"He had a jolly lucky escape," said Kimber.

"Senza dubbio."

"Giovanni," interrupted Tommaso, "you had better go quickly to your home and, without delay, get into your bed. Should the Tedesci come to search, it would be advisable for them to find you in bed." He turned to Kimber. "As for us, my *capitano*, we have a long walk before us. We must be away up into the mountains to a safe place of which I am aware. On Sunday, if your people send us the right explosives, we will try again."

"Is it far?" groaned Kimber.

"If we walk quickly—as we must—we should reach it by morning. Come, *capitano*."

"Arrivederci," said Giovanni courteously.

8

The Tedesci

COLONEL VON GOSLAR SAT UPRIGHT AND SURVEYED the top of his desk. Yes, it was bare and clean, not a strip of blotting-paper or a pen-rack remained. Methodically he opened each drawer and checked that each was empty. He himself had taken the contents from the drawers only last night, carefully allotting each file to its appropriate subject and watching closely while Sergeant Speidel and a corporal parcelled them up, sealed the parcels, and took them away. Each drawer had been taken from the desk, to make sure that no paper had slipped out and become hidden in the furniture. Then each drawer had been replaced. Von Goslar was quite sure the desk was bare and empty, but—a careful and efficient administrator—he checked everything.

He glanced around the room, along the windowsills and cornices, over the floor, and especially in the corners. Not a scrap of paper remained anywhere. From the walls, the official calendar, the notices and orders, the large picture of the Führer, had gone.

Satisfied with his inspection, Von Goslar pressed the bell. Almost at once there was a knock on the door, and as the colonel called "Enter," Sergeant Speidel came in, clicked his heels, and stood to attention.

"Everything has been packed?"

"Everything, sir, except six chairs, two tables, a kit

of tools, and the two radio equipments; also sufficient knives, forks, plates, cooking equipment, and bedding have been retained."

"The inventories agreed?"

"Yes, sir."

The colonel relaxed a little. "You may stand easy," he said.

Sergeant Speidel adjusted himself, and after a pause the colonel continued. "You have had your orders, but I will repeat the chief points. From now on nothing will be put in writing. This, I realize, is somewhat irregular, but these are special circumstances. All communications will be by radio. As you will have no code-books, messages will be sent in clear. You will be in charge. Under your orders will be two corporals and twenty-four other ranks, including three radio operators. You will keep a continuous watch and remain on guard until you receive the signal ordering you to destroy the bridge. This signal will be sent to you as soon as Divisional Headquarters are satisfied that the evacuation is complete. How complete this evacuation can be is not yet known. Our staff will assess the position hourly, and—according to the information they have—will judge when the correct moment has arrived. Therefore you will in no circumstances act until you receive the signal. On receipt of the signal you will collect all weapons and ammunition, load these into the four trucks, which are here waiting your orders. You will then destroy the bridge, order your men into the trucks, and then drive in convoy by route X 143. Is that quite clear?"

"Perfectly, sir."

"I am leaving at twelve hundred hours. We will meet again when you arrive at R.D. 60. When that will be depends on how long it is before you receive the signal to act and then retire."

Colonel von Goslar looked at the sergeant and felt confident all would go according to plan. The sergeant had been with him for more than two years, and Von Goslar knew he was trustworthy and highly efficient. He was a man who obeyed orders to the letter. The arrangements were sound and simple. Von Goslar did not see how they could go wrong.

"You have two radio receiving-sets and they are both of the best type, well tested, and highly reliable; even if one should go wrong you will be able to use the other. Having no transmitter, you will not be able to transmit, but that will not be necessary. You will retain a continuous listening-watch, keeping your sets tuned only to headquarters until you receive the signal—your order— to act. Have you any questions to ask me?"

"None, except . . ." The sergeant hesitated.

"Well?"

"When is the signal to be expected?"

"That is impossible to say. Our staff will endeavour to get as much material and as many men away as possible before ordering the destruction of the bridge."

The colonel rose from his chair and walked to the window. Yes, everything was in order, the orders were clear and definite, and Sergeant Speidel could be trusted to carry them out. He looked out of the window towards the bridge.

"It is to be regretted that we must destroy that bridge," he said slowly. "As that Roberto Conti ruffian said, it is a work of art. And the consequences for the town will be calamitous."

At the mention of Roberto Conti, Sergeant Speidel

could not prevent himself interrupting. "Whatever calamity comes, it is their own fault. They deserve it. They are unclean and inefficient." He added hastily, "Sir."

The colonel did not rebuke the insolence. He realized Speidel was a sound man, who thought only of the German war effort. He disregarded the sergeant's remark.

"There is no information of that explosion last night?"

"None, sir. As you said, sir, with our garrison so much under strength it was impossible to make a wide search of the countryside. The patrol sent out found nothing."

"I am convinced it was a trap," said the colonel. "The Italians, knowing how many of our garrison had left here—there is no doubt they do learn these things—exploded a charge, believing that we would send out patrols over a wide area and so leave the bridge insufficiently guarded. The partisans were probably lurking near here ready to attack, take over, and hold the bridge against us. When we sent out only one small patrol they realized we were not to be tricked."

Von Goslar turned again to the window and looked out. He was silent for a few moments, then he said thoughtfully, "It has not been unpleasant here; Fontana d'Amore has beauty, a certain charm; I shall be sorry to leave."

Much as he wanted to reply, Sergeant Speidel controlled himself. He detested sentiment, and the colonel was being sentimental—that was the weakness of these Bavarians; they were too much affected by music and art; a pity, because the colonel was a first-class soldier and Speidel respected him. To the sergeant, no beauty could compensate for Italian laziness; they were careless and untidy; also they were treacherous. And Speidel did not consider Fontana d'Amore beautiful. The buildings were all of different sizes and not arranged in orderly straight lines, some houses projected farther than others, and some were built at different angles to those around them. Even the colour wash on the walls was of different shades. No, Speidel could not see there was any beauty in Fontana d'Amore.

The colonel glanced at his watch. "I do not leave until twelve hundred hours. It is now only nine." The mention of the hour reminded him of the daily inspection. "You cancelled the parade?" he asked.

"I did—yes, sir."

"It will be the first time since we came here that there has been no parade. Each day between eight and ten we have had our inspection."

Sergeant Speidel did not speak; he felt such a remark was unworthy of notice. Yes, it must be admitted that Colonel von Goslar was being sentimental—a terrible thing to say about anybody, and a scandalous thing to even think about a German officer, but a plain fact.

Perhaps the colonel sensed the sergeant's disapproval, for he straightened himself, and when he spoke again it was in his usual official tone.

"I will now make sure that everything is in order. You will come with me."

Sergeant Speidel, realizing the moment of weakness was now past, came to attention. The colonel's change of attitude satisfied him; he was sure that everything would be found correct and that not even one fault would be discovered, but it was proper that a check should be made. It was an officer's duty to assure himself that nothing had been overlooked—that was systematic, that was efficient.

Speidel opened the door wide and, as the colonel marched through, fell into step behind him. They went from room to room. Everywhere was clean, and—except for one room which contained the two radio-sets and another where some bedding and cooking utensils were set out—empty. They reached the top floor.

"Correct," stated the colonel. "I will now check the exterior of the . . ." As he spoke he turned his head for an instant and glanced through the window. A man was crossing the end of the street. The colonel jumped forward. "Look! Is that——?"

The sergeant turned quickly. As he reached the window the figure disappeared behind a building to the left, but the glimpse had been sufficient to convince Sergeant Speidel. "I am sure! I can tell the way he moved, the way he shuffled!"

"After him!"

The sergeant sprang to obey the order, rushing down the stairs ahead of the colonel. As he ran out into the street he called to a corporal to come with him.

"To the left," he ordered the corporal. "Down that lane. Hurry. An Italian with dark glasses—hold him."

The sergeant himself ran straight ahead down the street at the end of which he had seen the figure disappear. As he reached the last building he stopped, pressed himself against the wall, and peered cautiously round the corner. The street to the left was deserted. Had the ruffian gone into one of the houses? Very well, there would be a search. . . .

Sergeant Speidel suddenly sniffed through his nostrils. A man had come from a lane about twenty yards away and was trotting towards him down the street. It was clear what had happened; the creature had gone into the lane, then, seeing the corporal at the other end, had turned back in a panic. Speidel drew back his head and remained rigid against the wall. He could hear the rapid footsteps coming nearer, louder.

As the man ran past him, Speidel leapt, his arms outstretched. There was a shrill scream as the man swerved away, and for an instant it seemed as if Speidel had missed the catch. Then his hand closed on Roberto's arm.

"I have you!"

For perhaps five seconds Roberto struggled to slip away, then as the sergeant gripped tighter and got his other hand on Roberto's throat, the scuffle ended.

"If you resist I will throttle you!"

Roberto could not speak; his mind did not function.

From the lane from which Roberto had come the German corporal was running towards them; up the other street that led from the building with the swastika over the door, Colonel von Goslar, if not actually running, was approaching rapidly.

"So," said the sergeant, tightening his hold again; "so, I have you—yes."

"Ow," Roberto wailed. "You are hurting."

Speidel twisted one of Roberto's arms behind his back, then as the breathless corporal arrived, he barked sharply, "His other arm—take it, and if he attempts to get away twist it harder."

"I am not trying to get away," Roberto managed to gasp. "It is not my wish to get away——"

"Silence," roared the sergeant. Then, as the colonel reached them, he jerked Roberto to a more upright position. "Attention!"

"It is he," said the colonel. "Yes, it is he."

"He was wearing dark glasses, sir. When I caught him

they were smashed, but his walk—that he could not disguise."

"So, Roberto Conti, you see we have you in the end. That is proper, that is as it should be."

Roberto was no fool. Terrified as he was, his wits began to work. "My colonel," he started, "there is some mistake. I was on my way to find you when this scound— this good sergeant intercepted me. I was coming to see you——"

"Bring him to headquarters," snapped Von Goslar. "Bring him quickly. There are faces at every window; we do not wish the people to be foolish and attempt a rescue."

"Sir, of that there is little chance. He is most disliked by the people of this town."

The colonel turned and began to march back towards headquarters. Speidel and the corporal, gripping Roberto between them, fell in behind.

"Colonel, my dear colonel, it is all a laughable misunderstanding. I was on my way to see you on a matter of importance. I wished to inform you of certain disgraceful things that were being said. I knew it was my duty to come to you at once, I wished to talk——"

"You will soon have an opportunity of talking to the correct persons—the Gestapo," said the colonel. "Bring him."

The three Germans marched briskly towards their headquarters, taking Roberto with them.

It was after eleven hundred hours. Von Goslar sat upright in the chair beside the bare-topped desk, two soldiers on each side of Roberto stood rigidly to attention; Sergeant Speidel, also standing to attention, stood slightly in front and to one side of the prisoner. Roberto, sweating and breathless, flopped between the two guards.

He had had an awful time. He had been subjected to the greatest indignities. They had stripped him to the skin and searched his clothes; they had questioned him most discourteously; they had accused him, many, many times of being a liar; they had shouted at him until he could not think—questions, questions, nothing but questions, and abuse. Several times it seemed as if the colonel was going to order Speidel to hit him. Worst of all, at intervals they ignored him, talking as if he were not in the room.

"This is too serious a case for me to deal with here," the colonel had said. "It is not just that when we last saw him he spoke derogatory words about the Führer; for that offence you, sergeant, could administer adequate punishment; but he has deserted his post. He was mayor of this town, acting under my orders, and, without permission, he abandoned his duties. That is serious. Desertion is a crime—even for an Italian—punishable by death. Also I feel he knows a lot more than he has said. We have not learnt where he has been hiding. Probably he could disclose useful information. The proper persons to obtain such information are the Gestapo; they have the implements and know just how much pressure to apply."

Sergeant Speidel felt slightly disappointed. It looked as if treatment of the prisoner was to be put into the hands of others.

"No," the colonel continued, "he will have to be taken back to Command Headquarters. I have not room for him and two guards in my car. So you, Sergeant Speidel, will bring him with you when . . . you understand me?"

"Yes, sir."

"You will keep him locked in the cellar. You may give him some food and water if you think it necessary. You will, at the first convenient occasion, deliver him to Command Headquarters. That is all."

"Remove the prisoner," roared Sergeant Speidel.

"You are making a great mistake," cried Roberto. "My dear colonel, you do not comprehend my loyalty, my enthusiasm for your cause. It is not that I would conceal anything from you. My love of truth is well known. It is just that I have nothing to confess. I am innocent, I know nothing, I——"

"Take him away," the colonel ordered. "He is a liar."

Half an hour later Von Goslar was getting into his car. The driver sat upright, staring straight ahead, apparently oblivious of anything around him. When the order was given he would drive the car; until that order came he was as silent and immovable as a motor before the current is switched on. Sergeant Speidel stood upright, holding open the door of the car. Von Goslar was saying a few last words to the sergeant.

"You have your orders. I am sure every eventuality has been foreseen and each action planned in detail. The bridge will be destroyed at the proper time, when you receive the signal. Then you and the men under your orders will—after you have deposited Roberto Conti at Command Headquarters, you will obtain a receipt for him—report to me at R.D. 60. You understand?"

"I understand, sir, but . . ."

"But?"

"If this Conti attempts to escape I may use what force is necessary?"

Von Goslar knew exactly what the sergeant meant.

Speidel was vindictive and hoped for an excuse to have his revenge. A statement that injuries to Roberto had been incurred during an attempt to escape could cover a great deal.

"He will not try to escape, and if he does it will be due to your failing to take proper precautions. You have sufficient men under your orders to prevent any attempt. When he is delivered to the Gestapo he must be undamaged and unbruised. The Gestapo are most particular that their prisoners arrive in sound condition—that is desirable for their purpose. You will not strike Conti— that is an order."

Resentfully the sergeant thought that his question had done more harm than good. If he had not asked . . .

The colonel relaxed a little. "It is satisfactory that we arrested that Conti before we left here; not to have done so would have been untidy, incomplete." The colonel stopped speaking for a moment. A lesson to be learnt by the arrest of Conti had occurred to him. He paused, contemplating, then continued, "We Germans are precise, we check thoroughly; if I had not gone over the building this morning—although that was not strictly necessary —I should never have seen that man through the window. If I had not seen him that Conti would not now be in the cellar." Then he added, "It is strange that he was out openly in the town, in full daylight."

"That can be explained, sir. While he was being taken to the cellar Conti expressed surprise that at nine hundred hours we were not engaged on our daily parade. Knowing that each day from eight to ten we always were so occupied, he considered it safe to lounge about the town. It has apparently been a habit of his to do so."

The colonel got into the car; Sergeant Speidel closed

the door and saluted; the driver resumed consciousness, the car drew away and disappeared up the road to the North.

To describe Roberto as being in a state of despair would be an understatement. If the late William Shakespeare had come to him and said:

> 'Art thou so bare and full of wretchedness
> And fearest to die? Famine is in thy cheeks,
> Need and oppression starveth in thy eyes,
> Contempt and beggary hangs upon thy back ...'

Roberto would have agreed that that just described the situation and his feelings.

The walls of the cellar were of solid stones, not just small stones that, if a man had plenty of time and the necessary tools, could be removed; but large blocks of stone, with plenty of iron-hard cement between them. The tiny window, out of reach near the ceiling, had thick iron bars across it—bars put there long ago, in the days when it was essential to keep such persons as men-at-arms and 'scurvy knaves' out of one's residence. Intended to resist a battering-ram or a small cannon, the bars would certainly keep Conti where he was. But to make doubly sure that their guests did not leave them, the Germans, who had used the cellar as a prison during their occupation, had bolted a sheet of strong steel grating across the window. The door was also one of those thick, massive barriers which were considered desirable in days gone by. And here, again, the Germans, who in their usual thoroughness took no chances, had bolted a large plate of half-inch steel on to the door.

Escape, Roberto realized, was just not possible. There was not one piece of furniture in the cellar, not one chair, or even a box; if Roberto became tired of standing the only alternative was to lie down on the stone floor. For over four hours, in an attempt to minimize his discomfort, he kept trying different positions, his final conclusion being that a sitting position, with his back wedged into a corner of two walls, gave the least pain.

Roberto had given up all hope. There was not the slightest chance of his survival. Escape from this room was impossible, and when the Tedesci did take him away he would be surrounded with brutes who would be glad of an excuse to murder him. If he behaved discreetly and gave them no such excuse the end of the journey would be the Gestapo. Roberto had heard many stories about the methods of the Gestapo, and in abject terror he tried to drive such agonizing thoughts from his mind.

That he would be subjected to violence and harrowing pain and eventually be shot seemed to Roberto a certainty. There was no way out. Well, then, he would be a martyr. He reminded himself of the courage with which some martyrs had met their end—that man who was put on a gridiron, for instance. Yes, if they did that to him he would die a martyr, a patriot murdered by his country's enemies. He would speak some wonderful last words, words that would go down through the ages, imperishable words that would forever be associated with the name of Roberto Conti.

If they tortured him he would not disclose anything —at least he hoped so. Father Leone's name must not be mentioned, Tommaso, who had been discourteous, Arnaldo, who had tricked him, even that insulting Maria, he would protect. When they heard how he had suffered to save them they would all their lives be ashamed, and smile no more. That would teach those creatures a lesson!

The thought of Don Leone reminded him of prayer. Prayers could work miracles; it was well known that sometimes miracles did happen. Anything was worth trying. He wriggled on to his knees and started to pray. As he prayed, using the once familiar formulas, the words he had known so well as a child, his insincerity seemed to leave him. He was no longer deceiving himself. For an instant he saw himself as he really was.

"You know what I have been," he prayed, "you know what I am, you know that if I had my time again I would be different. I do not ask you to save me, just . . ."

The sound of footsteps—loud, heavy footsteps—interrupted him; footsteps on the stairs. There was a rattle and click of a key turning in the lock; Roberto sprang to his feet; the door opened, Sergeant Speidel and two soldiers came in. The sergeant did not speak for a few moments, but stood glaring at Roberto in silence.

"So," he said at last, "we have you—yes? You see it does not pay to try to deceive us. In the end we catch you, and soon you will be confessing all to the Gestapo."

Roberto did not reply.

"Examine the room," Speidel barked at the two soldiers. "It is impossible that he should have attempted anything, but it is proper to check."

The soldiers went slowly round the room together, examining every inch of wall, floor, and ceiling.

The sergeant watched Roberto's face. "You have complaints—yes?" Then, as Roberto still did not speak, the sergeant shouted, "Answer me!"

"I would like a mattress and some blankets, also some wine. I do not feel like any food."

"No mattress or blankets will be provided; the floor is suitable for you. A jug of water will be brought at nineteen hundred hours. It is not intended to give you food or wine."

The sergeant waited for some protest, some pleading from the unhappy man, pleading that he would reject scornfully. None came.

"You are a traitor. I have known it from the first. You are a liar and a bombast, puffed up with pride. You are like all Italians—unclean and inefficient."

It was not courage but rather desperation that caused Roberto to leap forward. "And you," he shouted, "are a viper, a cur, a blackguard! You are like all Tedesci—a beast, a bully, a scoundrel! But you have lost the war and . . ."

Speidel drew back his arm to strike. Roberto did not, as Speidel expected, cringe. Then as his clenched fist shot out, Speidel suddenly remembered the colonel's words. "That is an order." He had been ordered to deliver the Italian unharmed and unbruised.

"Get out!" stormed Roberto. "Filth of the cesspool, get out!"

Speidel went stiff with rage. That this creature of all people should dare to insult . . . But the colonel's words "That is an order" hammered in his brain. An order was something his instinct, his nature, his whole life's training told him must never be disregarded. An order was to be obeyed to the letter, it was not to be questioned; one did not use one's own judgment, one obeyed.

"Come," he shouted to the two soldiers, "away before I . . . Outside!"

"Yes, go!" bellowed Roberto. "Go before I kill you all. Get out!"

The heavy door clanged behind the Germans, the key clicked in the lock.

Alone again, Roberto's fury did not cool immediately. He stamped round the room shouting abuse. A hunger to tear at something with his hands, to smash something to pieces, overwhelmed him. The walls, the door, the window, were impregnable. There was no furniture to break up, but in one corner of the room a strip of wood perhaps four inches wide was nailed across the junction of two walls. It ran from floor to ceiling. Wild to destroy something, Roberto sprang at the plank and tugged furiously. He got his nails in a crack; he heaved, unconscious of the pain. The crack became wider. Roberto prised two fingers in; the plank shuddered and then came suddenly away from the corner. Behind the wooden strip were two electric cables; one end disappeared through a small hole in the ceiling, the other end through a hole at the bottom of the wall. Still obsessed with his desire to destroy, Roberto gripped the two wires and heaved; they stretched; Roberto heaved again. Somewhere in their length a joint snapped, and the wires hung loose.

There was nothing more on which Roberto could expend his rage. Exhausted, yet somehow relieved by his purposeless destruction, he sank panting on to the floor.

Five minutes later discretion began to creep back into his mind. He did not regret that he had lost his temper and spoken to that foul sergeant as he had done. Roberto had nothing to lose, they were going to . . . well, yes, kill him anyway, and to have said those things had been satisfying. That the sergeant had not retaliated had been puzzling; he was a brutal beast, and to accept as he had done . . . Could it be that he was frightened? That he was a coward? Roberto had often heard it said—although experience had not always confirmed the truth of this— that bullies were frightened when faced with a fearless man of iron. A glow of pride began to warm Roberto. He had certainly spoken freely, he had faced the monster, and the monster had run away. Speidel had cringed. Yes, certainly, he had been terrified. The pity was that Tommaso and that Maria had not been present; it would have shown them how terrible Roberto could be when he was provoked.

Still, it was as well to be cautious. Perhaps it had been a mistake to tear down that plank. Roberto stood up and inspected the damage. The wires—they looked the kind used for an aerial or an earth on a radio-set—were hanging loose. Whatever their purpose had been, they were now useless. But the plank itself was intact. It had split in one place, but this would hardly show. Roberto decided there was no good purpose in annoying the Tedesci further. He tucked the wires back behind the plank, into the corner of the wall, and rammed the plank back into position. You could hardly notice, thought Roberto, that it had ever been disturbed.

9

The American

SERGEANT SPEIDEL HAD BECOME SERIOUSLY WORRIED. It was now nearly midnight and since eighteen hundred hours not one message had been received on the radio. Headquarters had remained silent. Yet Speidel felt almost sure that the fighting on the opposite side of the river was very near its conclusion; he even thought that it might have already ended; and still headquarters had not yet sent the order telling him to destroy the bridge.

Soon after dark truck after truck had appeared from the south and rumbled over the bridge on their way north. The trucks had been driven fast and had not stopped to identify themselves, but from a few shouted words as they passed and the marking on the tailboards Speidel had known them to be German. Later, when the passage of the trucks had become intermittent, there had been some bursts of heavy firing, the thud of large-calibre guns about four kilometres away among the hills to the south. Since then, at intervals, there had been the *tat-tat-tat-tat* of machine-guns, and some of these had sounded quite near, almost on the opposite bank of the river.

The sounds and flashes during the last three hours had seemed to Speidel typical of a well-planned withdrawal that had almost reached its conclusion. Surely there could not now be a large force remaining south of the river? Yet headquarters had sent no signal. Of course it was possible, thought Speidel, that a strong and still successful rearguard action was still being fought. It might be that, but . . .

He walked back into the building and into the room where two radio-operators, earphones clapped over their ears, sat watching the wireless-receivers. "There has been no signal yet, are you sure?" he asked.

One operator took off his earphones and passed them to an assistant sitting beside him. "Nothing. I am quite sure."

"Both sets are in order?"

"Both are in order. We have one set on batteries and one on mains. Both sets are working because we are getting a lot of mush, and from time to time some weak signals—too weak to decipher—that proves that our sets are in order."

"It is strange."

"Mush and weak signals are to be expected, because according to orders we are tuned in only to head-quarters."

Sergeant Speidel frowned. "There is no chance that you could have missed headquarters' signal?"

"That would be impossible. Because we are tuned in only for headquarters, when headquarters transmits it will come in loud and clear—unmistakable. We could not fail to hear it."

"You have never left the earphones?"

"Two of us have been listening continuously. No signal has been received, that is certain."

The suspense was beginning to make the sergeant feel quite sick. He was sure something had gone wrong. It was, he knew, insubordination to even think it, but he dared to wonder if headquarters had failed to . . . No, such an error was impossible, it would be inefficiency.

"The two sets are in order? Headquarters' signal would be loud and unmistakable? Two of you have been listening continuously?"

"Yes, sergeant, I am positive."

Speidel turned away and walked out of the building on to the road.

He was convinced that the fighting on the southern slopes had almost ended. Even the rattle of machine-guns had now ceased, and he longed to give the order that would put all weapons, ammunition, and men into the four waiting trucks. Then when the trucks were loaded and moving up the road to the north he would follow them to where the firing-switch stood by the roadside, ready to complete the circuit. Then he would press the plunger and destroy the bridge. He knew that the time had come when he should take that action, he was sure . . . and yet headquarters had sent no signal.

For one mad moment he contemplated acting on his own initiative, but the wording of his order had been clear. ". . . Therefore you will in no circumstances act until you receive the signal." No, he had no alternative but to wait for the signal. He was part of a great, an efficient, machine, a machine that never failed to plan in detail, and to operate as was intended. It operated because each unit, each man, obeyed orders to the letter.

All the same, he was certain that the last stand of the rearguard force on the hillside opposite was nearly over. Why had he not received the order to blow up the bridge? It was dangerous to leave it so long. Anything could happen—a sudden rush across by the British that would leave Speidel helpless and the bridge intact. Naturally headquarters wanted to postpone destruction to the last possible moment, but in the opinion of Sergeant

Speidel they were taking the gravest chances. It was wrong to allow such thoughts, it was almost mutiny, but he felt headquarters were making a mistake.

Standing there, peering into the darkness, he suddenly realized a vehicle was at the south end of the bridge. It seemed to stop, then moved slowly forward again. Speidel strained his eyes, trying to see it more clearly. It looked like an armoured car. Was it German, or could it be British? Things were so mixed up these days, each side using captured vehicles . . .

To Speidel's relief, when the car reached his side of the bridge it put on speed and roared past into the darkness up the road to the north. So it was all right, it must be German. Or could it be . . .

He stood for a few moments, undecided, then at the sound of the car stopping on the road behind him he turned his head. The armoured vehicle that had passed had pulled up about fifty yards up the road—just where the firing-switch that would destroy the bridge stood beside the grass verge. From the car jumped three men armed with Tommy-guns. As they dived for the cover of the hedge Speidel recognized British uniforms.

Two more armoured cars thundered across the bridge, then—safely across on the northern side—one swung round and stopped, so that it faced Speidel and the German Headquarters. The second car, with Tommy-guns poking out, pulled up in front of the building.

As the German sergeant dived for the shelter of the headquarters building, there came a spatter of bullets against the wall. Speidel, unhurt, leapt through the doorway. His hunch, he knew, had been correct. The fighting on the south side had finished. The bridge was intact, and the means of blowing it up was now covered by British guns. Headquarters had waited too long before sending that signal.

But, he thought with satisfaction, he had behaved correctly. He had obeyed his orders to the letter. He had been efficient.

The night had almost passed, and grey streaks of light in the sky to the east showed that dawn was near. Convoys of camouflaged vehicles were crossing the bridge and—to the drone of low gear—rolling away up the road to the north. A continuous stream of tin-hatted infantry, burdened with bulky packs and each man carrying a rifle in one hand, plodded past in single file.

Inside the building the Germans had used as their town headquarters an English major sat on the desk swinging his legs. Behind him lounged four soldiers, armed with Tommy-guns, who were guarding the prisoners. Sergeant Speidel, standing rigidly to attention, considered the major's attitude too informal. It was not correct for an officer to behave in such a manner.

Speidel had experienced no difficulty in understanding the instructions the British major had just given him because, in addition to speaking Italian, he had studied English and spoke it quite well. But, incidentally, had the Britisher been willing to disclose it, he spoke German, and also Italian, fluently.

"Well, that's all there is to it," said the major. "We'll be sending you, and the blokes with you, back for interrogation as soon as we've got spare transport going south."

He looked at the disarmed Germans and thought they seemed almost unconcerned—a bit puzzling, but you could guess what was going on in their minds. Higher Authority, they had decided, could not criticize them;

they had obeyed orders; they had fulfilled the duty allotted to them; now they were prisoners, they simply accepted the situation, and waited for further developments.

"Have a cigarette," the major said, holding out his packet.

Sergeant Speidel, still looking straight in front replied, "No. I thank you, but it would not be proper."

When would these British learn to behave correctly, to dress properly, and be smart? It was unsuitable for an officer to wear his tunic unbuttoned, and to disclose a knitted jersey underneath. Also he was not wearing a hat, and his hair needed cutting. It was disgraceful that a member of any army should go about in this slovenly way. And the Americans—why, they were even worse than the British; no discipline at all.

The door opened, and a British corporal came into the room. "The engineers have just finished stressing the bridge, sir," he said cheerfully. "They told me to tell you it will carry the weight O.K., and that the tanks are starting to come over now."

The major nodded. "Until we've got spare transport to run these Jerries back," he said, "we'll have to put 'em somewhere where they can't get out. I sent Sergeant Higgins half an hour ago to find a place."

The corporal looked behind him. "Here's Sergeant Higgins now," he said. "Seems in a bit of a sweat, too."

As the corporal stood aside the sergeant—a plump, red-faced man with a close-clipped moustache—marched into the room.

"Well, found anywhere?"

"I 'ave, sir," replied Sergeant Higgins briskly, although it did seem that he was somewhat disturbed. "The very

place we want, a cellar down below, door covered with
an iron sheet, double bars at the windows, couldn't be
better, but . . ." He paused as if uncertain what to say
next.

"But what?"

"Well, there's an 'Eye-tie' in there, and we'll 'ave to
get 'im out—that's certain—before we can put any
Jerries in. In my opinion this 'Eye-tie', sir, is off 'is rocker;
potty—if you get my meaning."

"Batty? Oh, well, we'll soon haul him out. What's an
'Eye-tie' doing there, anyway?"

"From what 'e said, the Jerries had locked him up there
some days ago; no food, no water——"

"That is untrue," Speidel interrupted. "Water was
provided at nineteen hundred hours."

"To my way of thinking," Sergeant Higgins continued,
giving Speidel a hard look, "this 'Eye-tie' is now a loony
—crackers. When I went in he thought I was one of the
Gestapo, a Jerry in British kit to trick him."

"Poor devil," said the major. "Must be as mad as a
coot."

"Yes, sir, that just expresses it. Claims to be the Lord
Mayor of this town. And, do you know," he added in-
formally, "from the way he keeps on talking, it might
well be true. I've met some of these town councillors at
times, when I was at home, and they go on just like this
'Eye-tie.' "

"Well, we've got to put these Jerries in, so get him
out."

Sergeant Higgins hesitated. Then he said, "If you say
so, sir, of course it can be done; but he's pretty awkward.
In my opinion it will need four or five men to overcome
him. You see, he's just plain nutty; ses he isn't coming

out for anybody; ses he's staying where he is whatever anyone ses."

The major stood up impatiently. "I'll come down and see him myself." He turned to the four soldiers behind him. "You're responsible for these Jerries. See none of them gets away. Come with me, Sergeant Higgins."

As the major strode through the door, Higgins spoke again. "I think we'd better take the corporal and two men with us, leaving two men to watch these Jerries will be plenty. But this 'Eye-tie' . . . well, I'm used to dealing with difficult cases, as you well know, sir, but, if you get my meaning, this 'Eye-tie' is a bit out of the ordinary run."

Across the hall, through the kitchen, and down the cellar stairs went the major. On the instructions of Sergeant Higgins, the corporal and the two men he had detailed to be in the party led the way. Sergeant Higgins brought up the rear.

"I'm glad you're taking over, sir," said the sergeant, making it clear where the responsibility now rested. "You speaking Eye-talian fluently, being bi-lingual, as the saying is, may be able to get some sense into this 'Eye-tie.' "

"Strong place, this," commented the major, as they reached the cellar door. "Just the spot to keep those Jerries until we can send them south."

The door creaked open. The five British stepped into the cellar. In one corner, his back pressed against the wall, stood Roberto Conti.

"Buon giorno," began the major. "Now look here, you've got to come upstairs with us."

"I am doing no such thing!" shrieked Roberto. "Do you take me for a fool? Do you want to kill me? I tell you I am staying here, I am not moving, I am not——"

"Take it easy, old man, no one's going to kill you. You're making a mistake, we aren't the Gestapo, we're British."

"I do not care what you are! There is nothing to choose between you. I will not leave this safe place. I am not going to die to please anyone; I am not suitable to die; I am not in a state of grace. I will not be killed until Father Leone has arranged matters that I do not go to hell. Even then it is not my wish to die——"

"Will you get it into your silly head that we are not going to kill you. We are British."

"You *are* trying to kill me. You are trying to take me upstairs out of this safe place. Here I am below ground; the walls are thick; I am in a shelter. Upstairs there would be no protection for me at all, and a terrible bombardment is going on. Outside shells are flying about—great, enormous shells of unbelievable ferocity. I am fearful. Any reasonable man would be fearful in this bombardment."

"There hasn't been a shell near here all night," said the major firmly, "and there won't be. The Jerries' lines are miles away up north, and they're getting back there as quick as they can. This town is going to be a backwater. All you can hear is our tanks and trucks going past."

Roberto wriggled more firmly into his corner. "I have myself been bombarded, in this room, here to-night, and you say . . . I tell you, here great shells came smashing against the window bars. See—the window glass is all broken! Some of these enormous shells entered the room. I tell you, I thought my heart would stop. I vowed—I, Roberto Conti, the Mayor of Fontana d'Amore—vowed that if I were spared I would go into a convent."

"Not one single shell——"

"The marks are on the wall over there. Look for your-self. Go and look at them. They were made by shells that entered this room through the window. I heard them fly over my head and strike the wall. I tell you, the bombardment went on for hours; I was bombarded savagely; great shells burst all around me. If it was like that in this safe cellar what is it now like upstairs?"

Sergeant Higgins intervened.

"I think I can explain, sir. When we first reached here there was a Jerry sergeant standing outside the door. Just to hurry him up a bit we let fly for a second or two with a Tommy-gun, and one or two bullets may have gone through the window. That's what he must be talking about."

"I have been in great danger, I have been attacked. For hours I have suffered a terrible bombardment, I have . . ." Suddenly the meaning of Sergeant Higgins's explanation penetrated Roberto's mind. "And it was you that bombarded me!" he screamed. "Beasts! Serpents of the earth! You shot at me, vile creature! You tried to kill me when I was not in a state of grace." He shook his fist in the sergeant's face. "Brute! Barbarian! And you have destroyed our bridge! Vandals! Dogs of the gutter!"

"No one has damaged the bridge," said the major, feeling here, at least, he was on safe ground.

"But you will."

"We won't. Why should we? We got here before the Jerries blew it up, and stopped them doing it. The bridge is O.K., and so are you."

Conti put his hands to his face. "If that were only true," he wailed.

"It is true."

"True?"

"Absolutely. Word of honour."

Roberto Conti stared at the major. Suddenly he knew the man was speaking the truth. A great wave of relief swept over Roberto—an emotional man in ordinary times. The past twelve hours had been an ordeal that had reduced his nerves to shreds, and now his self-control collapsed. He began to sob. Tears ran down his face.

"I say, you know," the major said awkwardly, "no one's going to hurt you. You can go home as soon as we've checked on your story."

"But the Tedesci—why did they not blow it up?" sobbed Roberto.

The major began to explain. "Well, actually that's not quite clear yet. They intended to, but were waiting for a radio signal that never came. Their radio went wrong, or something."

Roberto's mind was in a turmoil. He had been arrested, captured at a time when he believed he was safe; he had been treated brutally and had suffered intolerable indignities; without hope, he had waited for torture and death. Then had come that frightful shelling. He had, he remembered, lain flat on the floor and shrieked . . . Any man would have done the same under such a bombardment. Even he, Roberto Conti, had been a little frightened . . . well, not frightened, but, for a few moments, concerned—a little alarmed. He had rolled about the floor because that was the prudent thing to do. Yes, he had behaved wisely. And now not only was he safe and under the protection of his good friends the beastly British, who assured him the shelling had stopped and that Fontana d'Amore would not be a battleground, but the bridge was safe also. The bridge was intact and no longer in danger— and so was Roberto. Could a man ask for greater blessings? It *was* a miracle! Those vows of his had worked a miracle!

"My benefactor!" he howled, and leapt at the major.

Taken by surprise, the major was not quick enough to dodge Roberto's outstretched arms, and for a second or two he staggered, reeling in the Italian's embrace. Before he managed to heave himself clear Roberto had had time to plant two loving kisses on the major's cheeks.

"Here! I say, dash it all!"

Sergeant Higgins, who was a Regular with long service in the army, restrained his feelings, but the corporal and the two soldiers had not the same self-control. They laughed outright.

Roberto, as the protesting major pushed him away, laughed too—the happy laugh of a man who has good reason to rejoice.

It had been daylight for some hours, and the sunlight shining on the rippled waters had turned the river to a stream of silver. Vehicles and guns were still rolling across the bridge on their way north, but the long lines of infantry in single file had disappeared, and in their place parties of signallers unreeled lines of telephone-wire along the roadside, and worried detachments of engineers probed about searching for booby-traps. The steady drone of aircraft engines came from overhead—fighters, far up, guarding the sky.

Seated on a wall by the roadside, Tommaso Ucelli watched morosely the passing show. That the bridge had not been destroyed was highly satisfactory, that the efforts of the *capitano inglese* had been frustrated by so many things going wrong, and also that the Tedesci had failed to blow up the bridge, was undoubtedly a good thing. But Tommaso was worried. Somehow he felt a responsibility for this young Englishman. Tommaso had come to like him; he was so simple, so trusting, so much in need of guidance and protection. And Tommaso felt the *capitano* was going to need all the protection he could get. His superiors would be enraged; they would consider he had failed to carry out his mission; he would be disgraced; possibly they would send him to Russia, or at least confine him for life in a fortress. Worst of all, two men from London might come.

Tommaso looked at the people lining each side of the road: excited people, some with bunches of flowers, flinging handfuls of blossoms into the passing vehicles, waving enthusiastically, laughing. Occasionally there came a burst of cheering as some more unusual type of truck or gun rolled onward. It seemed to Tommaso that almost every one he knew in Fontana d'Amore was welcoming the—what was the word? Those armies that came . . .

"So, we still have our bridge intact," said a voice behind him. "And we are—so far—all alive. It is very satisfactory."

Tommaso turned his head. It was Arnaldo who had spoken. Tommaso nodded. "Speriamo," he muttered. "But let us not be too sure yet. These British have a way of muddling things. My confidence in them is not complete. During the past week I have been caused serious doubt. And now their armies are here as . . . as———" he paused; what was the word? ah, yes, that was it— "liberators. When an army performs this 'liberation,' usually every one is much worse off."

"That is true," agreed Arnaldo. "This 'liberation' we hear so much about seems to consist of firing shells at buildings and ruining the countryside. In my opinion people are placed in much discomfort when they are liberated."

Tommaso stared in silence at the rejoicing crowds. "Arnaldo," he said, at last, "I am concerned about the *capitano inglese*. He went about half an hour ago to try to arrange with his people for a conveyance back south to what he calls H.Q. I do not like it."

"The *capitano* . . ." began Arnaldo; then, as a figure detached itself from the people by the roadside and came striding towards them, he finished, "He is coming now."

"All O.K.," said Kimber, when he reached them. "I ran into a sapper colonel I once knew slightly; he's going back to Terni and will give me a lift in his truck. I can hitch-hike a lift on from Terni all right."

"And that is what you wish?"

"Wish? Oh, yes, most convenient; it all fits in. The sapper's going to pick me up in about half an hour."

Tommaso looked at Kimber gloomily. This *capitano* was like a child—so trusting, so heedless of danger.

"I do not think, *capitano*," Tommaso said slowly, "I do not consider, you are wise. You have enraged your superiors with a message that was impolite, and you did not blow up the bridge as you were ordered. To me, it seems most indiscreet to return to your people."

"What? Oh, that will be O.K. Probably a bit of argy-bargy at first, but they'll soon cool off. 'Time the great healer,' and all that, you know."

"*Capitano*, listen to me. Why do you not stay with us here? You can be in the hills, you will be kept most secretly, my organization will look after you. You would be safe and happy. Why go back to meet the rage of these infuriated superiors? Stay with us for safety."

"You would be a most welcome guest," Arnaldo put in. "Giovanni, Don Leone, or myself would rejoice to hide you, and if anyone came asking for you he would be sent away quickly, and if he proved obstinate he would have his throat cut and the body removed without a trace. Stay with us, *capitano*, in peace and contentment."

Kimber stood there trying to frame a reply. He knew they meant well, that they were concerned for him, and he was touched by their kindness. How could he make them understand?

"I can't stay here. Don't you see it would be—well, desertion, and all that."

"Better desertion than Russia," Tommaso said solemnly. "*Capitano*, don't you realize——" He broke off suddenly, as he saw a girl push her way through the crowd on the opposite side of the road and pause in the front row of sightseers. "Francesca!" he cried. "Francesca, it is my Francesca!"

Arnaldo surveyed the people. "Yes, it is Francesca Camerata. She would be well advised to be cautious crossing the road. The drivers of these vehicles are not as careful as they should be, and if she were knocked down and run over it would, for you, Tommaso, overcast the liberation."

The girl waited until there was a gap in the moving traffic, and then started to hurry across the road.

"Francesca," called Tommaso, "be careful. Francesca . . ."

As she reached the middle of the road, tripping towards them, suddenly a loud whistle—a 'wolf' whistle—shrilled out. The girl hesitated, turned her head. Tommaso leapt into the air like a startled partridge.

"What was that? Who did that?" he screamed. "That

whistle—I heard it. It is an insult. Who whistled, who . . . ?"

Francesca, safe across the road, strolled towards them.

"Francesca, I demand to know who whistled! I will cut his throat, I will . . ."

Francesca smiled shyly. "Buon giorno," she said. "Ah, Arnaldo, and you, Captain Kimber."

"Never mind anything," roared Tommaso, glaring backward and forward at the crowd, his head turning like the lamp at the top of a lighthouse. "Who made that filthy whistle?"

"I do not know. I have no idea. See, here is Father Leone coming to speak to us."

"Don Leone? It could not have been him," said Tommaso, who, consumed by jealousy, was still a fair-minded man.

Father Leone joined the party. "It is good to see you all safe," he said, "and our dear bridge as it should be. It is a happy day for us all. . . ."

"Some one has whistled at Francesca! I will kill him. Whistled, a disgusting whistle, at Francesca. I will not have it. It is torment, it is past bearing. I will kill him."

"You are probably imagining things," said the priest soothingly. "Probably it was intended to guide one of the vehicles, or you just imagined it. I heard nothing."

"I heard it," said Kimber. "A bit annoying."

"I heard it also," supplemented Arnaldo.

"On a happy day like this," Don Leone urged, "why let a trifle spoil our happiness?"

"Annoying! Is that what you call an insult? Spoil our happiness! Let me tell you, I am not happy, I do not want to be happy. Foul creatures whistling in that way after

Francesca." He turned on the girl. "You must have encouraged him. You must have given him cause to behave in that way."

Francesca Camerata had a temper too. She turned and faced her fiancé. "How dare you! How dare you suggest . . ." She almost choked. "As if I were . . ."

"No man would whistle after a girl unless she had encouraged him."

"I do not feel that is accurate," commented Arnaldo. "It is the way she walks, it is her figure. Men seeing her become excited."

Tommaso flung his two clenched fists above his head and spluttered with rage.

"On a day like this," began Don Leone.

But Francesca had heard enough; she also had lost her temper. She whirled round. "I am going. I never wish to see you again, I despise you, Tommaso Ucelli. You are vulgar, you have disgusting thoughts, you are vile, you are . . ." As she started to walk away the whistle came again—loud, clear, decisive.

"I think," said Arnaldo, who was the first to speak, "I think it was that monk on the wall over there. I was looking that way, and I saw him take his fingers from his lips."

"A monk!"

"The one with the white robes, with his cowl over his face; the one sitting on the wall; I saw him . . ."

"Monks, priests, popes!" howled Tommaso, "they are all the same. Never did I think to see Holy Church degraded by such creatures. When I get——"

"Tommaso," said Don Leone sternly, "control yourself, you are making a scene. I will go across and question that monk; it is unbelievable that he should have——"

"He has got off the wall," Arnaldo intervened, "he is coming towards us."

It was true. The white-robed monk was now skipping across the road, dodging the traffic.

Francesca paused, hesitated.

"Hiyah, toots," called the monk.

"The *Americano!*" shrieked Tommaso. "It is the *Americano*. Let me get at him!"

Don Leone skipped nimbly in front of the furious man. "Quick," he cried. "Quick, Arnaldo, *capitano*, hold him, get hold of his arms."

The four men swayed from left to right, Tommaso trying to push first one way then the other around the priest, who blocked his path. Arnaldo and Kimber tugged at Tommaso's arms in an effort to restrain him.

"Hello, folks!" Sergeant Tuttle greeted them as he reached the struggling mass. "Hiyah, Francesca."

"How did you get here?" asked Kimber, using all his strength to hold back Tommaso.

"On a scooter. That monastery place didn't suit me— no, sir—I jest despised it. I wasn't staying there—no, sir —not while I had my health and strength. So this morning, when a guy—some sorta tradesman, I guess—arrived on a scooter an' parked it outside the gate, I soft-shoed out, gave that scooter the once-over, and said to myself, 'Bob Tuttle—scram!' Yes, sir. Jest followed the signboards back here."

"But you couldn't," Kimber panted. "You'd have had to come right through the retreating Boche troops and our crowd after that."

"Sure, that's jest what I did do. Easy as fallin' off a log! When I met any Jerries I jest raised my right hand, like I was sorta blessin' 'em, and said kinda solemn, 'Dominus vobiscum'—yeah, 'Dominus vobiscum'—Latin stuff I picked up from a dame I got acquainted with in Baltimore. And, oh boy, did it work! Ask me! I guess those Jerries were tickled pink to meet a guy from a monastery ridin' a scooter and handin' out this 'Dominus vobiscum' stuff. Maybe they were surprised too, kinda dumbfounded. Anyway, they were in a hurry, hell-bent on a getaway, an' they did not click. So Bob Tuttle jest kept on scootin' and hollerin' 'Dominus vobiscum.' But when I started comin' through your outfit I kinda changed my talk. I hollered, 'Keep it hot, you Limeys! You're dynamite! Attaboy!' An' that sure did git the laughs. They thought it rich to see a monk on a scooter, hollerin' that way."

"Will you stop him talking!" shouted Tommaso. "His voice enrages me."

"So what?"

"How did you get those clothes?" Tommaso howled. "Did I not tell you, Arnaldo, to tell the monks to take away his clothes? You have betrayed me, you have disobeyed my orders. Two men will come from Turino and——"

Sergeant Tuttle laughed. "Takin' my clothes away! Say, that's old stuff. I knew my way round that one when I was in college.

"We can't hold him much longer," gasped Arnaldo.

Don Leone, who was now exerting his whole strength to restrain Tommaso, nodded agreement. "The American must leave Fontana d'Amore immediately. It must be arranged at once. Tommaso will murder him."

"I will, I will," stormed Tommaso.

"Is that so? Lemme tell you . . ."

Kimber, getting a firmer grip on Tommaso's arm, spoke

quickly. "I am leaving. That sapper colonel will be waiting now; there will be room in the truck; I can take Sergeant Tuttle with me."

"Tommaso, you hear that," said Don Leone. "The
American is going, he will not see Francesca again, he
will leave now. All is satisfactory. Tommaso, control
yourself I implore you."

"Can you hold him there?" asked Kimber, "while we
do a bolt for that truck?"

"It is doubtful," Arnaldo panted, "but we can try. If
Father Leone gets a firmer hold . . ."

"Come on," said Kimber, to the sergeant, "quick as
you can to that truck over there. Run like a hare while
they try to hold him. Do as I say."

As the two men ran towards the waiting truck Kimber
turned his head. "Thanks a lot," he shouted. "Good show.
Thanks for everything, and—good luck, Tommaso."

"Aw, zipper your kisser," said Sergeant Tuttle.

10

The Square

MORE THAN NINE MONTHS PASSED BEFORE ROY
Kimber came to Fontana d'Amore again, and
then it was only the merest chance that caused
him to make the visit. He was on leave, on his way south
intending to break his journey and spend the night at
Terni, when trouble developed with the car he was driv-
ing. Realizing that the trouble necessitated a garage and
several hours' work, and that if he attempted to push on
the engine would fail altogether, he consulted his map
to find a town or village where the repairs might be
carried out. Experience with army repair depots caused
Kimber to distrust them, and in any case the nearest
depot was at Sienna; so a wayside garage seemed to be
his best chance of a quick repair. The map showed Fontana d'Amore about eight kilometres away, and Kimber,
deciding that the devil he knew was better than the devil
he didn't know, turned his failing car towards Fontana
d'Amore.

On the outskirts of the village he came to a house with
an open shed beside it, in which two men were working
on a dilapidated vehicle. Some battered enamel signs
indicated the place provided petrol and repairs to "all
makes of cars." A newly painted notice announced "English conversed"—a statement that Kimber considered
might be somewhat inaccurate.

The owner of the garage, however, proved efficient,
and quickly discovered the cause of the trouble, but, as

Kimber had feared, the cylinder head would have to come off, and the repairs would take several hours. Kimber learnt it would be midday to-morrow before the car would be ready. The man managed to make it clear that he would have willingly continued through the night, but the electric light was not working and the few oil lamps available would be inadequate and unsafe. "Also," he explained, "there is in the village this evening a great ceremony. A ceremony of the greatest importance, signore, and it is essential that I and my brother here should attend. Such a ceremony as has not taken place in Fontana d'Amore since before the war. It is necessary I and my brother should be there, signore. But have no fear, to-morrow morning we will start upon your car."

"You don't just mean *domani?*"

The garage proprietor was offended. "Certainly I do not mean *domani*, I mean to-morrow. By midday you shall be on your way. I am not the sort of man who says *domani*."

Kimber inquired if he would be able to find a lodging for the night in the village, and the man assured him that he would.

"Senza dubbio. There are many most comfortable hotels. You will be well cared for. But there is an English major still in our town, and he would advise and welcome you. He has been many months here in charge of the military arrangements. He leaves to-morrow. He has stayed to see the ceremony in the square to-night. To-morrow he leaves. His quarters you will find easily; they are at a house on the left as you enter the town."

"I think," said Kimber, changing the conversation, "that I have met you before. Just under a year ago.

Wasn't it you who came one night with a battery to the bridge? I was there, with Tommaso Ucelli."

The garage proprietor was a cautious being, he never answered questions unless he understood their purpose and could assess the possible consequences of his reply. Now, much as he wanted to shake Kimber's hand, welcome him to Fontana d'Amore, and press him to have a glass of wine, he restrained the impulse. "I think, signore, you may be mistaking me for my cousin. He had much to do with batteries and often took them to assist persons whose cars had broken down." Then, with a cheerful smile, he added, "Do not concern yourself about your car, signore. It will be ready and in perfect condition by midday—and the cost will be small. I am sure you will find a comfortable hotel in the town. Buona fortuna."

Kimber was not much concerned about finding a room for the night, although he felt the statement about there being many most comfortable hotels was not true. If he could find Tommaso or Arnaldo he knew they would put him up, and if they could not be found hospitality from Don Leone was a certainty. Arranging to return for his car about midday, he set off walking.

Fontana d'Amore seemed to have suffered little damage, the fighting to have by-passed it. The familiar narrow streets were unchanged: iron balconies—occasionally washing strung out on a line between them—open doors showing the dark interiors beyond, the colour-tinted walls of the buildings—faded pink, cream, and pale blue. From some of the open windows came the blare of music from the household radio. Children played about the doorways. It was almost as he had known it months ago.

He had no difficulty in finding the town major's

quarters. Two prominent notices on the gateposts of a villa, standing back from the road, announced in English and Italian that here was the British Representative. Some packing-cases neatly stacked by the front door, obviously waiting collection, indicated a removal was in progress and that the major and his small staff were almost ready to leave.

The major proved to be a pleasant fellow, glad to see his guest, and anxious to be helpful.

"Yes, I'm finished here. Leaving in the morning. I'd have gone a week ago but for this show they're having to-night. It's a bit of a bore, but H.Q. felt we'd better be represented at a 'do' like this. Sort of show good feeling, and that."

Kimber nodded.

The major continued, "Sure you don't want me to fix you with a room? Sure you can fix it yourself? Only wish we could put you up here, but all packed up ready to go, you know. You see the mess we're in, don't you? Well, let's find a drink."

Over a drink they exchanged reminiscences and discovered mutual friends. After some time talking of acquaintances in the army they began to speak of the people of Fontana d'Amore.

"Tommaso Ucelli?" said the major. "Oh, yes, he's in fine form. I like him. He got married about a month ago —darned pretty girl called Camerata, Francesca Camerata. I went to the wedding. Jolly fine show it was; a terrific crowd at the church. The priest, Don Leone— did you know him?—he did them well; special blessing from the Pope, and all that sort of thing. We had a grand party afterwards; marvellous what they can do with things, as short as they are. But, I say, when you were here, did you find some of the wine pretty drastic? No doubt about it, some of this Italian wine is most deceptive. Even affected me a bit. Yes, we had a good show. Bit of an argument towards the end with an old girl called Maria, who seemed annoyed about Ucelli being married in the church, or something like that. I didn't quite understand what it was all about."

"Was a fellow called Arnaldo there?" asked Kimber.

"Arnaldo Vivarelli? Ah, yes, he was best man. He and a chap called Giovanni got pretty festive. Giovanni's a jolly good sort too—would be an asset to any party— kept wanting to sing old Tuscan songs. In the end he tried to dance on a table, and his wife took him off home."

"Did you ever come across Conti—Roberto Conti? He was the Fascist mayor here."

The major seemed surprised by the question. "Good Lord, yes! Roberto, why he's been acting under my orders while I've been here, sort of running the civil side of things. We kept him on as mayor. Actually he wasn't a great deal of use. Bone idle. I've been chasing him up nearly every day about something. 'Why hadn't he done this,' or 'Had he done that.' But really he's not a bad sort; talks a lot of hot air, I know, and does damn all, but still you can't help liking him. This show to-night in the square is really for Conti. It will be his big moment."

"His big moment?"

"Yes. We've put a bronze plaque up on that wall in the square—the wall with the cornice on the top—and to-night Don Leone is going to unveil the plaque. There'll be a band, and the whole town is turning out. You know how they love any sort of celebration and a lot of noise. The plaque's sort of in honour of Roberto."

Kimber looked at the major in amazement. "Roberto? A plaque? Are you sure? I don't understand it at all."

"It's not all that difficult," the major explained. "You see, for about a month after I took over I didn't have much to do with Roberto. I rather ran things myself. Then one day General 'Bibs' came through here on his way north; they were moving H.Q. right up north by this time, and 'Bibs' stayed here an hour or two looking into things and talking about this and that. Towards the end of his visit he said, 'Now there's just one thing more. I shall have to do something about this Conti feller. I read the reports myself and made a note of it at the time. I suppose I ought to try and get him some sort of a decoration, but that won't be easy, and perhaps I can find some simpler way. You see the feller and find out what would please him. He seems to have deserved recognition of some kind, so get him fixed up and send me a report of what you've done.' I just said 'Yes, sir,' and the next day I saw Don Leone and told him our general wanted Roberto to have something. Don Leone suggested some kind of memorial. So that's all there is to it. We got a plaque made in Firenze and put it up. It's being unveiled to-night."

Roy Kimber sat trying to sort out the story, to reconcile it with the facts as he knew them. He felt bewildered. "But Roberto," he said at last, "why did 'Bibs' think he should have a decoration? What on earth had he done?"

The major pushed some papers aside impatiently. "Well, he did save the bridge, didn't he? Destroyed an aerial or something when he was in prison, and so the Jerries never received the wireless signal. He saved the bridge."

"Why, I was sent here to destroy it!"

"Yes, I heard that. But strictly off the record, I under-stand that was a bit of a blunder, a bit of muddled think-ing. It would have held us up for a week or more if it had come off. Anyway, when you and the Jerries didn't man-age to finish the bridge it was a godsend to us."

"Do you mean they *didn't* want the bridge blown up?"

"Well, actually, no. It helped us no end when we were able to use it."

Kimber sat in silence for a few moments. "Let me get this straight," he said at last. "They did *not* want the bridge blown up?"

"No, I've told you, the whole idea was a bit of a 'mix up.' "

Kimber stared in bewilderment. "So they sent me here, and if we had brought it off . . ."

"Well, you know how things are," the major said soothingly. "Annoying, and all that, of course, but, well, these things do happen, don't they? Anyway, you'll come to the show to-night, won't you? Join the official party, and all that. We're meeting at Don Leone's house at seven-thirty and going on from there."

Kimber drained his glass and then stood up. "It beats me. It just beats me altogether. A decoration—well, a plaque put up on a wall—for *saving* the bridge. For us to have stopped the Jerries blowing it up would have been about half the job we took on trying to blow it up ourselves. When I think of all we did and . . ."

"It's no good fretting, old boy. Anyway, the show's to-night; eight o'clock prompt. Not that I expect the 'Eye-ties' will be prompt, they never are. Probably start nearer nine. Still, seven-thirty at the priest's house. See you there."

Roy Kimber nodded, and, somewhat amazed, walked out of the headquarters, and turned towards the town.

Roberto stood shuffling his feet on the worn carpet in the priest's room. If the room had been bigger he would have paced backward and forward, and he felt a vague resentment that at a time such as this he should be limited. This was no time for a man to be hampered by chairs and tables, it was a time for space, space to stride freely, to march triumphantly, to fling out his arms.

"Careful!" exclaimed Don Leone, as a sweep of Roberto's hand just missed a statue of St Joseph on the mantelpiece. "Be placid, be calm. You are becoming nervous."

"Nervous! I, nervous? You do not know me, Don Leone. I, who have faced the Tedesci and defied them, I, to whom this so beautiful plaque with the memorable words, the imperishable words upon it——"

"Strictly speaking, you should not have seen the words upon the plaque until it was unveiled. I fear, Roberto, you have been prying. I told the workmen to keep the plaque covered and secret. They told me you had several times been there, lifting the sacking and peering underneath."

Roberto did not trouble to reply to the accusation. His mind had already travelled on to the picture that had recently been so often in his thoughts—the picture of himself, Roberto, standing in the square beside the wall with the so beautiful cornice; the people of Fontana d'Amore gathered to honour the man who had saved their city; of the women who would gaze at him admiringly, and wish that in the past they had behaved differently and been more kind, more accommodating; of the men—

and also that Maria—who had misjudged him, who had dared to be disrespectful. For such creatures it would be now humiliation, if they were capable of shame. Now they would cringe.

There was that Tommaso—in the past he had behaved far from well. There were times when he had not been courteous; and Arnaldo, deceiving his own brother-in-law and forecasting calamities that never happened—no, Arnaldo had not behaved properly; also, that *capitano inglese*, a rough, uncouth creature, who well deserved a sharp lesson; it was undoubtedly heaven's intervention that had sent that *capitano inglese* to Fontana d'Amore just when he would see Roberto honoured and proclaimed. Then there was this English major, with his constant "Has this been done?" and "When are you going to do that?" The man had been like a troublesome mosquito. And then there was Don Leone—consider his conduct how you liked, it had not been worthy of a priest; leaving Roberto for days alone upstairs in a miserable room not fit for—but worst of all was that Maria! Roberto's mind flamed with resentment when he remembered some of the things she had dared to say. For Maria—a hen like that—to speak in such fashion was outrageous!

Now he would show them all, he would repay the debts with abundant interest. When the time came for him to make a speech, when Don Leone had unveiled the plaque, when a deep silence came on the awestruck people, he, Roberto, would stand up before them as the saviour of their city. Yes, 'city'—for was not Fontana d'Amore just as important as Rome? A fig for Rome! Then he would speak. Before the listening multitude, he would say what was in his heart. He knew exactly what he would say, he had written his speech out most carefully, many times. He would be dignified. Yes, he would be dignified. He would thank the people for the plaque. He would tell the people again how he had saved their city.

He would recount how, imprisoned alone, waiting for death, he had thought only of ways to frustrate the Tedesci; how, regardless of death, with great cunning he had destroyed the aerial and earth wires, so that no radio signal had been received. Then, still speaking with dignity, he would tell of these curs who had slighted him; he would speak of them with contempt, and expose their despicable conduct to every one. What would that Maria feel when she heard him call her publicly "a fat old sow?"

"You must not upset yourself," said Don Leone. "It will be a simple ceremony. There is no need for concern. I will explain to the people, I will show them what their feelings towards you should be. You will see, all will come right, everything will be forgotten and forgiven. It will be a happy occasion for you."

Roberto wondered for a moment what the priest meant by "forgotten and forgiven." There was no necessity to forget. Roberto did not want the people of Fontana d'Amore ever to forget what he had done. But he dismissed the words as meaningless. Priests talked like that, half the time no one could understand what they meant.

There came a loud knock on the outer door, and Maria, who had been hovering about in the hall, opened it quickly. The major and Roy Kimber had arrived. Don Leone rose to welcome them.

"Others not come yet?" said the major. "It's close on seven-thirty."

"They will be here soon," replied the priest. "It is good to have you here, and you, *capitano*. It is a happy night for us all."

Don Leone turned to pour out wine for the newcomers, and Roberto pushed the glass he had emptied across the table. The glasses filled, the priest went on speaking.

"Our town has been saved from a great disaster, and it is right that we should celebrate. We have been granted a wonderful blessing, and we must thank God for the mercy shown to us."

"And unveil that plaque upon the wall," added Roberto.

"Yes, I am glad about the plaque. It will remind the people in years to come how near Fontana d'Amore was to oblivion. That we should have had a ceremony of thanksgiving and a celebration is certain, but it is due to you"—the priest inclined his head towards the major —"that the plaque will be upon the wall."

"Oh, I don't know," said the major, somewhat embarrassed. "Had to do something, and all that."

"It was a kind and charitable thought."

Roberto was not sure that he liked the way the conversation was going. All this talk of blessings and thanking God; that sort of thing was right in its proper place; it was natural that a priest should talk that way, he had to do so, it was his profession. But it was he, Roberto, who had saved the city. The ceremony to-night was to acknowledge in public, before a great crowd, the debt the people owed him. A little more about every one's indebtedness to Roberto would have been more seemly.

The conversation continued, and from time to time Roberto joined in, but on the whole he said little. He told himself he should be cynical and aloof. These were three

of the men who had, in the past, not treated him with the
respect that was his due, and whom he intended to expose
before all the people of Fontana d'Amore. In a little time,
an hour at the most, they would be cringing with shame,
despised, objects of scorn. He, Roberto, was in no mood
to treat them now as friends. Long ago he had heard a
story of a nobleman, surrounded by his enemies, who
knew that soon help from friendly allies would appear,
that these enemies would be crushed. That nobleman had
remained silent and contemptuous. Through half-closed
eyes, with a lazy laugh he had flicked a speck of dust
from his immaculate linen. That was how he, Roberto,
was behaving—unconcerned, indifferent, until the
moment came to humble these creatures.

Roberto glanced down through half-closed eyelids.
Then, noticing a soup stain on the lapel of his coat, he
moistened his fingers at his mouth and scratched at the
spot.

"I say, Conti," said the major, turning to him, "expect
you're feeling pretty bucked, and all that? Naturally a
bit nervous, of course, but——"

"Nervous!" Roberto interrupted swiftly. "What is all
this talk about nervous? Every one keeps talking about
nervous. I, Roberto Conti, nervous!"

"Sorry. Just thought you seemed a bit jumpy—sort of
fidgety."

The words stung Roberto. Here he was, silent and contemptuous, cynical and unconcerned, and this detestable
major called him fidgety.

"Was I nervous when the Tedesci were here? Did I
not face them alone? Did the Tedesci not cower before
me?"

"You were jolly lucky," said Kimber reminiscently,

"What I can't understand is why that Hun sergeant—what was his name—didn't kick you all over the place. What was the fellow's name?"

"Sergeant Hermann Speidel," supplied the major. "I came on his name a lot when I was going through the 'bumph.' "

"That's the fellow—Speidel," Kimber chuckled. "He was going to kick Roberto backward and forward across the square."

Furious, Conti could have struck these two imbeciles. To talk at a time like this, and in such a manner, was abominable, when they should have been showing respect to the hero—yes, hero—who had saved the city. On the very night when he, Roberto Conti, was to be honoured, when it was to be acknowledged . . . With a great effort he mastered his feelings. "It is my grief, my great grief," he said, "that Hermann Speidel is not here to-night. If he were he would hear and see the people acclaim me, he would cringe and cower with shame. But perhaps it is for the best. If I were to meet him again it is possible that I might not be able to control myself, that I should strike him many times, as I did before." Then, with simple dignity, he added, "On a great night like this it would be unseemly."

"I say, you know," said the major, "aren't those fellers coming? It's after eight."

"They will be here soon," the priest assured him placidly.

As he said it there came the sound of footsteps and a sharp knocking on the door. A few moments later Tommaso and Arnaldo were in the room.

"The square is full," said Tommaso, when the preliminary greetings were over. "Packed, and people at

every window. You will have the biggest congregation,
Don Leone, you have ever had."

"To me, such acclamation will be embarrassing,"
Roberto said. "That all the people should wish to show
their gratitude is natural, but to me, who am of a modest
disposition, it causes———"

Arnaldo interrupted. "It is the band that has brought
them," he said confidently. "Yes, it is the band."

"My people," Don Leone explained to the two Englishmen, "they all love music. They are happy when they
are together and there is music."

"Or any sort of noise," added Arnaldo. "We Italians
are fond of noise."

"That's true," said the major, "I've noticed it myself.
When an 'Eye-tie'—I'm sorry—an Italian—is pleased
with life he generally bangs away at something. I've seen
a feller just sitting there banging a dustbin lid."

Roberto listened to this frivolous conversation in dis-
gust. This was no time to be talking of trivialities, of
bands and noise; it was a time to be talking of plaques
with imperishable words upon them, and of the man
whom the plaque honoured. Well, these soulless beings
would learn, when he, Roberto Conti, stood up and made
his speech to the people; yes, they would learn.

"I say, what about getting on? Getting a bit over time,
isn't it?"

The priest stood up and marshalled the party. "You
and I, Roberto," he said, "will walk together in front.
Then if you, major, will walk with Captain Kimber, and
you, Tommaso, with Arnaldo. We go out into the square,
and then across to the wall on which is the plaque. Walk
slowly and in a dignified manner. The Carabinieri know
what is needed, they have been instructed, and will keep

a path clear to the wall. I shall then speak to the people
and, finally, draw away the curtain covering the plaque.
After that the band will play, and we may enjoy ourselves."

"You have forgotten one thing," said Roberto; "after
the so beautiful plaque is unveiled it is natural that I
should, as Mayor of Fontana d'Amore, tell the people
what this day and this plaque means to them. When you,
Don Leone, have unveiled the great tribute, I will address
the people."

Arnaldo shook his head. "I do not think that would be
wise. The people will want the band and will become
restive. If you try to make one of your usual speeches
they will——"

At that moment the band in the square started to play.
It was a large band, for many Italians were musicians
and there was no difficulty in obtaining plenty of volun-
teers. It was a band with many brass instruments—many
cornets, many trumpets, two Sousaphones—and three
drummers. The tune being played was *Funiculi, Funicula*,
a tune that invited energy, and gave ample scope for the
clashing of cymbals, the *boom-boom* of the drums, and
the throb of the Sousaphones.

In the priest's room conversation became impossible.
While the four Italians seemed unconcerned by the
terrific din, the two Englishmen were stunned.

"The noise to end all noises," shouted the major to
Kimber.

Kimber nodded.

Following signs from Don Leone, the party moved out
of the house. As the front door opened, the music hit
them like a blast.

Down the narrow lane, crowded by people who had

overflowed from the square, went the party. *Funiculi, Funicula*, roared the band; crash, crash, *Funiculi, Funicula*.

If the Carabinieri in the square had ever tried to keep a way clear to the wall where the unveiling was to take place they had long since abandoned the attempt. The people were packed solid. Above, at every window, were people, whole families crushed together leaning out, and, although the thunder of the band seemed certain to terrify any child, white-haired grandmothers danced young babies on the window-sills. Enthusiastic, enraptured, the people basked in the deafening uproar.

With great difficulty Don Leone and Roberto managed to push their way through the good-humoured crowd until, breathless and somewhat dishevelled, they reached the wall. A few minutes later Tommaso and Arnaldo managed to join them. The two Englishmen, stunned by the noise and the crowd, gave up the struggle and succeeded—to their discomfort—in finding a place in which they were pressed against the side of the bandstand.

Suddenly the musicians saw the priest standing by the wall, and, just as suddenly, they stopped playing. For some moments the sound continued to echo among the buildings.

"There has been a mistake," Don Leone said to Roberto. "They were not to play until after the unveiling."

Roberto, still breathless and indignant after his struggle through the crowd, snorted agreement.

"Help me up," said the priest. "I will speak to them standing on the bandstand. It had been arranged there should be a platform for me to stand on, but it has, I suppose, been forgotten, so I shall have to use the bandstand."

"It is unpardonable," said Roberto. "Having to fight our way through the crowd like that, and now no platform. It is undignified."

A dozen willing hands pushed Don Leone up on to the bandstand. Roberto clambered up after him.

There was complete silence for a few seconds, and then Don Leone began to speak. "This is a great day for Fontana d'Amore, and it is proper that we should celebrate it."

How true, thought Roberto, that is what should be said.

"God intervened and saved us from a terrible disaster," continued the priest. "I need not tell you, my very dear people, how overwhelming that disaster would have been, had it been allowed to come upon us. You realize the misery that would have followed better than I do. Many of us—but not perhaps as many as should have done—have already thanked God, in our church, for his mercy; many of you were at the Te Deum we were permitted to have in thanksgiving."

Roberto's attention began to wander. He looked down and saw Tommaso's and Arnaldo's upturned faces looking up at him. He looked at the faces in the crowd, identifying many of them. These were the people he had grown up with, some he had been to school with, played with as a child. They were his people, and they were seeing him, Roberto Conti, standing in the square, above them. They were looking up at him. In their minds they would be saying. This is the man who saved Fontana d'Amore and our bridge. The thought of the bridge caused Roberto to think of his mother, of how she had told him of his father first speaking to her of marriage upon that same bridge, and how she would never cross it after his death, but went round over the stepping-stones.

"But," the priest was saying, "there is a man here to whom we all owe much. One you all know well, and like."

Roberto wriggled with satisfaction.

"One who suggested this plaque should be erected, to be a reminder in the years to come of the saving of our town. I refer to our good friend, the English major."

The packed crowd howled enthusiastically.

This is preposterous, thought Roberto, Don Leone is getting senile. But somehow, to his surprise, Roberto found he was not now really angry. He kept looking at the smiling faces below him, and his resentment to those who had treated him disrespectfully lessened. Did it really matter? Here was he, Roberto Conti, standing up before every one, in the square, against the wall with the so beautiful cornice, not, as might well have happened, with a firing-party in front of him, but with a mass of his friends wishing him well.

The priest was saying something about Tommaso and Arnaldo, and the crowd howled their delight again. Then he went on, "And finally there is Roberto Conti. I know that in the past many of you have felt distressed by some of the things he has done. It would be untrue if I were to pretend we have always approved of his behaviour. But let us realize that by saving our bridge he has made reparation. Even his worst enemy must admit that it is through his action that we are here to-night, celebrating the saving of our homes, our soil, our livelihood."

Roberto felt himself trembling. What was being said, so publicly, before all the people, was true. Without him

Fontana d'Amore would now be a ruin. All these people around him were hearing. . . . A wave of affection, of good will, swept through Roberto.

"Therefore, I say to you all, whatever evil has been in the past should be forgotten. We should now remember only the good this man has done. Enmity is an evil thing. To keep in our minds memories of a person's bad actions is sinful. It is the duty of us all to forgive, and forgiveness necessitates forgetting. Let us all now start afresh. Whatever has occurred before this night, let it be forgotten. I say to every one here, He that is without sin among you, let him first cast a stone . . ."

Roberto did not like these references to the past. At a time like this they were unseemly. But somehow all his anger, all his resentment, had disappeared. Now, overcome with emotion, all he could think of was his love for every one. Every one? Yes, even Maria. He saw Maria standing below him, her face turned towards him, her face still grim and unsmiling. But what did it matter now? He, Roberto Conti, was honoured, acclaimed, he was above petty angers. As Don Leone urged, he, Roberto, would forgive and forget—forgive every one. There was only one desire now in his mind—to stand up and, in a great speech that would always be remembered and talked about, tell these people of his love for them all. In this great speech there would be no cutting references to the *capitano inglese*, no rebuke for Tommaso, Arnaldo, or Don Leone. No, not even for Maria.

Don Leone was coming to the end of his discourse. "And now," he concluded, "the time has come for me to unveil the plaque." He turned, and, after a moment's hesitation, bent down and spoke to Tommaso. "The cord, quick, the cord," he said. "I need the cord to pull aside the covering."

"The cord," shouted Tommaso, "pass the end up here."

Some people in the crowd, pressed against the wall, seized the cord, and handed it towards the bandstand.

"It is not long enough," said Arnaldo. "It will not reach. Stretch out a little farther, Don Leone, while I hold you."

"It will not reach because the platform was forgotten," said Roberto. "Had we been standing, as was arranged, upon a platform against the wall . . ."

"I will climb down," Don Leone said, and began to clamber over the side of the bandstand.

People below stretched out hands to help him. Some one in the swaying crowd stumbled against the man who was holding the cord. There was a tearing sound, and the curtain covering the plaque fell down. The plaque was unveiled. All might now read the imperishable words upon it.

Unveiled by some stranger, some unknown person in the crowd, but what did it matter, thought Roberto. All that mattered was that he should now make a great speech; never before had he felt so sure that his words would ring through the ages. What he wanted, what he must do, was to tell all these good friends of his how much he liked and loved them.

He turned to face the multitude below him, and swept wide his two arms.

The bandsmen, who had been waiting, uncertain of the procedure, took the gesture as a signal for them to start. *Crash-crash* went the cymbals, *bang-bang* went the drums, *Funiculi, Funicula* blared the whole band.

Stunned by the din—a din beyond his power to control

—Roberto stood helpless. "Funiculi, Funicula," roared the crowd, in time to the throbbing of the Sousaphones. For a few moments he stood hesitating. A speech? Not even the Duce himself could have competed against that band. His mind made up, Roberto turned quickly. "Help me down!" he shouted, and began sliding down the side of the bandstand.

What he now wanted, and what he was now going to do, was to push his way through the crowd to that so beautiful plaque, and read, once again, many, many times, those imperishable words.

> In 1944 Fontana d'Amore was
> in danger of annihilation, and
> the surrounding countryside of
> being laid waste. By the blessing
> of God, one of our people
>
> ROBERTO CONTI
>
> was given grace to avert this
> catastrophe . . .

At this point Roberto always went back to the beginning and started all over again.

IT ALWAYS RAINS IN ROME

by JOHN F. LEEMING
author of *The Natives Are Friendly*

A hilarious account of what happens at the end of the war in a small Italian town when the townspeople discover that their fourteenth century bridge is about to be blown up by overzealous liberators on the one hand and a retreating enemy on the other. The destruction of the bridge would cause the river to flood, destroy the soil, and reduce to rubble a work of great beauty. Into the conflict come all the personalities of the town: the Fascist mayor, the Communist partisan, the determined priest, and the equally stubborn German and British military, plus the inevitable *Americano*.

The mayor, despised by the people and the Germans alike, seeks a secret parley with the partisans, and asks them to persuade the British to frustrate the German plans. The Communist partisan leader is deeply suspicious of this ap-

(*continued on back flap*)